Self Published

Copyright © 2012 by Dana Grubbs

E-mail: captaindanagrubbs@yahoo.com

All rights reserved

This book is a work of fiction. Names, characters, businesses, organizations, places, events, and incidents either are the product of the author's imagination or are used fictitiously. Any resemblance to actual persons, living or dead, events, or locations is entirely coincidental.

ISBN 978-0-9851899-1-4

PRINTED IN THE UNITED STATES OF AMERICA

First Edition-Volume two

# THE WITCH'S HUT

This book was written with both the young and young-at-heart readers in mind. My hope is to return back to a time when one could read an exciting tale of adventure and intrigue without the overtures of drugs and sex that seem to be present in much of our society today. The thought for the story line came to me thanks to my granddaughter, who loves to read and sail with me when visiting over her summer vacations.

I created over twenty-nine illustrations for this book and I hope they will help bring the story to life as the reader lives the adventures page-by-page.

# Chapter 1

Friday

The time is 6:30 a.m. and the Boeing jet is winging its way across the sky. This is not the first time Gabriella has flown. She travels to Chile to visit her grandparents on her father's side at least once a year, so air travel is something she's well-accustomed to. On this trip she finds herself once again with her good friend and sidekick Susan Maddox. They are on their way to Bonaire in the Netherlands Antilles (a small island about fifty miles off the Venezuelan coast) to meet up with her maternal grandfather, Jack Elder, who has sailed his 41-foot sailboat Gypsy Wind down to the

**GABBY**　　　　　　**SUSAN**

island. Gabriella and Susan plan to spend the summer on Gypsy Wind, sailing in and around the waters surrounding Bonaire.

Gabriella Varde, known as Gabby to her friends, is the daughter of Angela and Cristian Varde. They live in Stone Mountain Georgia.

Gabby loves the outdoors and has had the opportunity to try a number of activities, some of which a normal sixteen-year-old girl would not customarily participate in. One summer in Chile she went bird hunting with her paternal grandfather, shooting two pheasant while they were on the wing (in the air). Snow skiing and water skiing have interested her as well, but nothing has captivated her excitement as much as scuba diving, which she is able to do on these long summer trips with Jack on Gypsy Wind.

Susan is quiet and, unlike Gabby, not the outdoors type, but they get along very well. Spending last summer on the boat with Gabby and Jack has allowed

Susan to discover a zest for adventure she never knew she had.

Gabby and Susan are classmates, and have known each other for the past five years. Best friends, they seem to grow closer every year. They plan to attend the same college after high school as well. Both girls have a strong background in languages and hope to be able to use that to their advantage in whatever fields they choose for their futures. Susan looks forward to another summer with Gabby and Jack on Gypsy Wind.

Friday 2:25 pm

Jack Elder is anchored just off the downtown pier in the town of Kralendijk, the hub of industry for the little-known island, as well as its largest city.

The trip to Bonaire took Jack four months. He started from the Florida Keys and worked his way down, island hopping from the Bahamas to the

Dominican Republic, and then to San Juan. Jack was in no hurry, wanting to enjoy every anchorage to its fullest. Once in San Juan, he hooked up with other cruisers heading for Aruba in a flotilla. Many cruisers like the "safety in numbers" method when making long passages at sea. Jack took on a crew member for that long crossing, to help with watches and handling the boat. Once in Aruba, Jack's crew member left the boat. Then Jack headed for Curacao, then on to Bonaire.

Jack, a retired Eastern Airlines pilot, has been cruising for several years now, and has become accustomed to the slower lifestyle. He's kept himself in excellent physical condition for a man in his late fifties. He attributes his health to the new lifestyle he has adopted for himself, having time to eat correctly. Working around the boat is totally different than sitting behind the controls of an Eastern Airlines Airbus. To fill his time while traveling, Jack oil paints and, on occasion, plays guitar in bars and restaurants.

Even though he has a nice little nest egg set aside, he likes to subsidize his income from time to time. He even has paintings for sale to fellow cruisers.

Jack is looking forward to having Gabby and Susan aboard for the summer. Sailing single-handed can be very lonely at times, so the company will be a nice change. The girls have sailed with Jack before, during their summer break a year ago. He knows it will take very little to get them back up to speed handling Gypsy Wind under sail.

Jack climbs into the dinghy, unclips it from the toe rail, fires up the outboard motor, and heads across the water to the dock. He needs to get to the airport to meet the girls, and is hoping their flight is on time. He has rented a small pickup truck to use while on the island and he keeps it parked next to the customs office, a white two-story building with large glass windows located next to the town pier. The customs office is the central point of the waterfront. Anyone entering the harbor must check any firearms and pay the entrance fee. Overnight stays require another fee, based on the length of the boat. Most of Bonaire is surrounded by a Marine Park and dropping the anchor rather than tying up to a buoy can lead to hefty fines for violators. But the main duty of the customs office is to control imports coming into the island, and making sure all documentation is complete.

Jack motors to the dock and ties up next to Karel's Beach Bar. Karel's is located at the end of the pier and many of the cruisers gather there during the evening hours for drinks and social time with each other. It's a great place to watch the incredible sunsets over Klein Bonaire (a small island just off the main island, known for great dive sights and reachable only by boat).

Bonaire is a rather small island compared to most, and the Flamingo International Airport reflects that. The check-in area is completely open to the weather and has limited seating. It's not a place one lingers for very long. Jack parks the truck and walks to the snack bar where large windows overlook the ramp as well as the runway in the distance. "No plane yet," he thinks, although ramp personnel are in place with the ground equipment needed to work the plane once it arrives. He sees an Air Jamaica jetliner land on a distant runway. The plane taxies to a pre-determined spot directly in front of his viewing window. The ground crew converge on the parked airplane like ants attacking food dropped to the ground. A set of stairs are pushed out and the door of the plane swings open slowly, allowing the passengers to disembark. After about ten minutes Jack sees Gabby and Susan making their way down the stairs, heading to the customs area and baggage claim.

After about thirty minutes, Gabby and Susan emerge into the public area of the airport , with their baggage in tow. They spot Jack immediately. "Hi sweetheart," Jack says, as he gives Gabby a big hug. "I sure have missed you." He turns and repeats the process with Susan and they make their way to the truck. Jack puts the baggage in the back. Gabby looks at the truck then at Jack, "This would have to be the weirdest looking truck I have ever seen," she says. "Ya," Jack agrees, "but it gets the job done." The truck is a Toyota with a front and back seat, and four doors. The bed of the truck is not much bigger than the length of a scuba tank. These trucks are perfect for divers to load tanks and gear into when heading off for a day of shore diving. Many dive resorts include a truck in their vacation packages, which allows guests to hit the road at any time of day (or night) to visit their favorite dive sites.

On the way to the boat, Gabby and Susan visually take in the island. This is their first trip to Bonaire and they really don't know what to expect. Gabby had read a little bit about the island before the trip and knew it fell into the category of a desert island with cacti, iguanas, small trees, underbrush, flamingos, and strangely enough, donkeys, which roam wild and are protected by the islanders. The island became a center for raising sheep, goats, pigs, horses and donkeys in the late 1500's. The locals were more interested in the animals for their skins rather than as a food source for the population, so the animals were allowed to roam wild around the island. Today only the donkeys remain wild and roam the island at will. Many travelers to the island leave unwanted change or cash at the airport in large clear glass containers before departing. The money is donated to the "Save the Donkeys of Bonaire" Foundation, which tends to the health and well-being of the animals. Visitors can even adopt a donkey of their very own, and get a report on the animal's health throughout the year.

  Jack drives through the center of town, which is a one-way street less than fifty yards long, with colorful buildings on either side. He continues down the street and then turns left heading toward the waterfront, but not before having to stop for a donkey grazing along the side of the road. The girls look at each other and start laughing out loud. Taking another left, the girls find themselves riding along the water's edge. "Hey, I see Gypsy!" Susan points as they approach the main docks and the restaurant area. This is where Jack had left the dinghy as well.

He decides to unload the baggage at the dock and leave the girls with their things while he brings the dinghy around. Bonaire, although very beautiful, has a lot of petty theft. If you don't want something stolen, you'd better not leave it unattended or it will be gone. The local police seem uninterested in the problem. Even the car rental center suggests leaving the car doors unlocked, to make it easier for the thieves to break in. The rental center seems more interested in the windows of the truck not getting broken than in their customers' possessions. Jack understands their position, as he knows how expensive it is to import car parts to the island. He parks the truck at the customs office and walks the short distance back to the dock.

Gabby and Susan packed rather light for sixteen year olds, and wisely used soft-sided dive bags for

suitcases. The flexible bags will be much easier to store in the boat than conventional hard-sided suitcases would be. Each girl has two bags, and Jack is able to load the bags and the girls into the dinghy all at one time. Once they arrive at the boat, the girls get into the cockpit and he hands the bags up to them. Then the girls take it all below and get started stowing their possessions. Jack remembers the last time they sailed with him, off the Georgia coast to the Florida Keys. "Hey kids," he yells, "how about not storing your under garments in the food locker this time?" He hears the girls laughing up front. On the last trip Jack kept finding the girls' things all over the boat. They had run out of room in the vee-berth and had stored items anywhere they could find room. He jokingly called them chipmunks, hiding their possessions all over the boat much like chipmunks might do with nuts before an oncoming winter. This time he had made some extra room for them in the hall locker, and he hoped that area could accommodate any extra items they might have brought along.

It is now afternoon and the girls want to go into town and look around. "Gabby," Jack says "That sounds like a good idea, why don't you two check out the town and in the morning I'll give you a tour of the island." Gabby and Susan jump into the dink, (which is the nickname given to the dinghy). "Gabby," Jack says, "take the radio and remember channel sixty-nine, just like we did last year." The girls make their way across the water to the dock, locking the dink to the pylon for safe keeping while they are on land.

Gabby and Susan are in their element since most Bonaire locals can communicate in English, Spanish, Dutch and papiamentu (the local dialect). In order to graduate from school in Bonaire, a student must be able to maintain a conversation in all four languages.

Gabby and Susan walk up the dock to the street which runs along the waterfront. Directly across the street from the dock is what some of the locals call the mall. The mall consists of nothing more than a walk-thru from the waterfront to the main one-way street Jack had driven down on the way back from the airport. The girls walk through the mall, with shops lining the walkway on either side. They pass a photo processing center and camera shop, a jewelry shop, an ice cream shop, and a few other places. They can tell the few cruise ships that stop at the island each month have had an influence.

The island is mostly sustained by the tourist dollar, but it still has salt as one of its main exports. As the plane approached the island, Susan had pointed out the large white salt mounds to Gabby, along with a huge pier which is called the Salt Pier. The girls walk the streets looking in the windows of many shops but do not enter any of them. Gabby points then says, "Susan look, it's a Kentucky Fried Chicken. Can you believe that?" Sidewalk cafés are found on every corner and street vendors line every nook and cranny anywhere room to set up a table is available. Gabby notices that most of the items sold on the sidewalks seem to be handmade, and the girls stop and admire many things while making their way down the street.

It doesn't take long to walk the town, and the girls find themselves back on the water front. "Gabby," Susan says, "Why don't we get an ice cream and sit on the patio and people watch for awhile?" "Sounds good to me," Gabby responds. They walk to the little shop next to Kentucky Fried Chicken and order two ice cream cones. Out in front of the Kentucky Fried Chicken is a small seating area that is shared by all of the restaurants in the mall. Each table has an umbrella to knock off the hot late afternoon sun. The girls settle down and realize they are both a little tired. Neither had gotten much sleep the night before due to the excitement of their upcoming trip. "Susan, I don't know about you, but I'm tired. What about you?" "Me to," Susan says, as she puts her feet up on the extra chair to rest them. "It's no wonder though, we started early this morning and flying takes it out of me. Why don't we finish the ice cream and head back to the boat? I think I could use a nap." Gabby agrees. "I think that's a good idea."

The girls sit quietly watching locals and tourists alike rushing in and out of the mall, while listening to a mother and her two kids speaking in Spanish at another table.

One of the children wants some chicken and the mother is trying to explain she can't afford it, telling them to drink their cokes and they can eat when they get home. Gabby and Susan look at each other and

realize life on a beautiful little island might not be as great as one might think with few jobs available, low salaries, and a high cost of living.

# Chapter

# 2

"Good morning Gabby," Jack says as she climbs the main hatchway ladder into the cockpit. Jack is an early riser and has been up for several hours already, having his morning coffee. "I thought you two might be sleeping in this morning. Would you like something to drink?" Gabby thinks for a moment then says, "Thanks, I would love some orange juice if you have some." "I thought you might like some, so I went shopping before you got here and picked up a few things I knew you two liked." Gabby sits down while Jack goes below for the juice. The morning is quiet, with only a few local fishermen heading out in their wooden boats for a day of fishing. Jack returns and the two sit quietly enjoying the moment.

Gabby, who is no stranger to moving around Gypsy Wind, notices something hanging off the main mast, some sort of bag. After pondering the question for a while she asks, "Granddaddy? "Yes?" "What is that thing hanging off the main?" "Well that's a little invention I made for us." "What is it?" Gabby asks. "It's a solar shower!" Jack has a proud smile of accomplishment across his face. "Ok," Gabby says, "I'll bite, how does it work?" "Well it's very simple actually. All you do is fill it with fresh water or rain water and hang it up where the sun light can get to it. The sun heats the water as it hits the plastic bag. The sun has not been up long and the bag is nice and warm already. I thought you and Susan might like to have a warm shower this morning." "Cool," Gabby says, "that would be nice, thanks." Later Susan is up and Gabby relates the story of the shower. "Won't everyone see us on the deck?" Susan asks. "Well I guess so," Jack says, "That's why I would suggest you wear a bathing suit."

The morning drags on and after the girls start looking a little bored Jack suggests they all hit the road and take in the sights. "You girls had better bring some water, and your bathing suits. Better yet, why not wear the suits and just slip on a pair of shorts over them?" Once in the truck, Jack heads north toward his favorite dive site, Thousand Steps. He has logged many dives at this site over the years. A local dive shop in his home town back in the States used to run group trips to Bonaire every year. He liked the short swim required to reach the reef and drop off at this location.

At most dive sites on the island, the swim to the reef is a hundred yards or better. This site is the exception, and the reason why many divers like it so well (not to mention the abundant sea life in the area). This is one of the sites where Jack has had the best luck locating the ever- elusive frogfish, which is a master of camouflage.

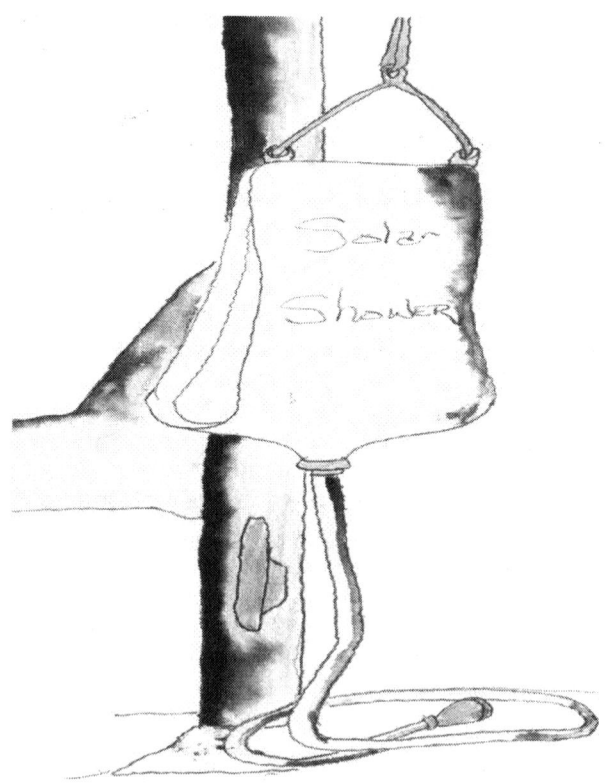

As Jack winds his way through town and into the outlying areas, the small brightly colored stores give way to homes. However the exterior color selection seems to remain the same. "Why is it," Jack thinks, "that regardless of the island, the dwellers always seem to like the bright colors to paint their homes? Could it be the bright colors reflect the sun's heat better?" The road takes a hard right and heads upwards along the coastline. They see homes built on the side of the mountain as they head further north. Steep cliffs line one side of the road, with deep caves cut into the walls. On the other side of the road, the waves crash against the rocks below. The road can hardly be considered a two-lane. If an oncoming car or truck should appear, one has to give way and let the other squeeze by the best way they can.

As they round another curve, Jack pulls over and parks in a sandy place. Tucked off the road and all alone is what looks to be the remains of a small house. "Granddaddy, why in the world would anyone want to live way out here?" "Well sweetheart, there is quite a tale that goes along with this place. I thought you two might enjoy seeing it, as well as hearing the story

behind it. Your mom told me you did a paper for school about the occult and voodoo." "Yeah, but the teacher wasn't impressed," Gabby says. "I don't think she was into that sort of thing. Susan and I worked hard on the paper and did a lot of research on the subject and all she gave us was a low B." "Well, add this to your research," Jack says with a smile.

"The locals call this place the Witch's Hut. Back in the early 1920's, a newlywed couple, Andrea and her husband Carlos, built the house you see over there." Jack motions to the walls standing in front of them on the hillside. "They lived alone way out here, far from anyone. Carlos would fish and capture iguanas for food. They also had a little garden alongside the house, probably right where we're parked. Anyway, Andrea had a baby girl and named her Shania after her great-grandmother. Things could not have been happier in the modest little home. One day Carlos went to town to sell some fish and some handicrafts that Andrea had made, hoping to make some money. The trip into town on foot took several hours. This was the day Carlos had been waiting for, the beginning of the Festival of Dia Di. Many people would travel into the towns of Kralendijk and Rincon on this day of celebration, giving Carlos a better chance to get top dollar for his goods. While Carlos was gone, a boat came ashore, more than likely right on that sandy spot over there," Jack points to a strip of sand across the road and down at the water's edge. "The couple had noticed a schooner anchored offshore the night before, and could hear the sounds of drunken sailors drifting across the water during the night. Carlos and Andrea didn't mind, many times a ship had dropped anchor along these shores and the sailors meant no harm."

Knowing he had the girls' full attention now, Jack continued. "The tale has it that sailors from the schooner came ashore while Carlos was gone and went up to the house. Andrea was alone except for the child. She could see the men moving closer to the house. Going out to greet them, she soon realized she was in danger. The men grabbed her, pulled the baby from her arms and dragged her into the house. When Carlos returned that evening, he found his wife dead on the floor inside their home, and the baby was gone. He noticed the schooner was no longer anchored offshore. Barefooted, he ran all the way back to town. With his feet bleeding, he walked from house to house until he found someone to help with the search for his baby girl. Later it was discovered that a schooner known as the *The Black Veil*, out of Jamaica, had been in the area. It was captained by pirates, who were known to pillage around the area from Aruba to Bonaire and the Venezuelan coastline. Slaves were of great value, and a girl-child could bring big money on the mainland. Why the pirates killed Andrea rather than kidnap her was never known. Perhaps she fought to the death, protecting her daughter, then the pirates took her baby.  Sometime later, Carlos, after realizing his baby girl was gone for good, traveled to see Andrea's great-grandmother Shania, who lived on the other side of the island in the town of Rincon.  Her years were unknown but everyone knew they numbered more than one-hundred.  The old woman had seen a lot in her day, and every year during the Festival of Dia Di she would share that history with the children - stories of the salt fields and the slave huts and the hardships endured in the early years of the island.  Carlos asked the old woman what he should do.  She looked deep into his eyes as if to see into his very soul, then told him to leave the island and never return.  He was to go to Venezuela to search for his child.  Shania would cast a spell that would mark the baby for all time, making her easier to find.  The mark would be in the shape of a cross on the child's neck, in plain sight for everyone to see.  Also, she would place a spell on the pirates that had kidnapped her granddaughter. This spell would be a living hell on earth, a spell that would replay itself over and over until the end of time. An evil spell such as she had promised her own great-grandmother years before she would never use her gift for.

The old woman was known for most of her life as a good and kind woman, well-versed in the voodoo cult, but never using her gift for evil. Many islanders would come from miles away to receive her blessings for a good crop, a healthy child or a safe journey.

After Carlos had departed the island, the old woman traveled to the now empty home of her granddaughter. Entering the house she could still see the blood stains on the floor. The old woman was heartbroken, and more determined than ever to get revenge. She set to work casting her evil voodoo spell. She cursed the house for all time and set it on fire while still inside, screaming the voodoo curse at the top of her lungs. The house became engulfed in flames and still she continued dancing within the walls of the humble cottage as it burned. The last words anyone heard from her were the names of Andrea and Shania. The old woman called the names of her lost granddaughter and great-grandchild until the flames subsided.

Many curious villagers came to see what the old woman had done. Only the charred walls of the house remained. The old woman was gone, never to be seen or heard from again. She had simply disappeared. There was no sign of her burned body inside the ruins of the house. Some think because she had broken her promise never to use her gift for evil, she was forever lost in the afterworld. And some think she haunts the house to this day. Anyone entering the house falls on bad luck, within a short time period. The locals never come near the house because they fear that bad luck will befall them. Local fishermen claim they have seen candles burning in the windows late at night as they sail their fishing boats past ruins of the humble little house. Some fishermen even offer a prayer as they pass, that the young Carlos found his daughter, unharmed and well. As for the pirates, legend has it that wreckage from their ship, *The Black Veil,* can be seen washing up on the sandy beach in front of the burned-out home every year during the Festival of Dia Di, which is the anniversary of Andrea's death and Shania's abduction. Perhaps this is an offering of penance from the pirates, or maybe it is a part of their curse, for them to relive the horror of a sinking ship year after year throughout eternity. No one knows for sure."

Jack looks at the girls without smiling and says, "Well, that's the story, to be believed or not, but understand this. I don't go inside the house and I don't want you two doing it either. I've heard stories of divers who have, and unexplained things have happened to them before they left the island."

Gabby and Susan get out of the truck without saying a word and walk to the front door of what's left of the little cottage. Jack remains in the truck. They look at each other as if waiting for the other to walk in. Nether girl moves toward the door. Instead, they back away and walk across the narrow road down to the water's edge, to the sandy beach Jack had pointed to earlier while telling the story. It seems almost like they are looking for wreckage from the schooner. "Gabby," Susan says, "That sent chills up my spine, how about you?" "You bet," Gabby replied. "I sure would like to know more about the story though." "Well, maybe later," Susan says. "I think your grandfather is ready to head out."

The girls go back to the truck and climb in, and Jack puts it into gear. The truck starts to move slowly, and they can hear the gravel underneath the tires grinding as he pulls onto the road. Gabby can't help but look back at the remains of what once was a happy home for a loving couple and a new child. She thinks to herself, "Voodoo and legends. Maybe, and maybe not."

Jack continues down the road and around the many curves to the Thousand Steps. He parks the truck and the three start down the steep rock steps toward the water. Susan starts counting each step out loud. "Susan," Jack says, "I don't think there are a thousand steps here." "Then why do they call it Thousand Steps?" she asks. "Well I don't know," Jack answers. "I guess it's because at the end of your dive you have to climb back up them with all your gear on to get to the truck. By then it probably feels as if there are a thousand steps here." "Ya," Susan agrees, "I guess you have a point." The three of them walk around in the small cove for a while and then head back up. Gabby and Susan find themselves a little winded once they are back at the truck.

Jack turns the truck around and heads back down the road, backtracking the way they had come. "Why are we turning around and going back the same way?" Gabby asks. Jack answers, "The road turns into a one-way just a little farther up the road. If we commit to it, we have to go all the way around to the other side of the island to get back to town. I want to head back into town now and take you toward the Salt Pier, to see if we can find a flamingo or two up around the salt mounds."

As the truck reaches the Witch's Hut Jack slows down, knowing the girls will want to take a final look at the walls that remain. "You know Granddaddy, I think I would like to know more about that story you told us." "Sure sweetheart, that might be fun," Jack says. Gabby thinks for a moment and says, "Do you think they have a historical place where we might be able to research the hut?" "You know," Susan says, "It would make a great paper later." "I don't know about that," Jack says, "after what you told me about the grade your last teacher gave you two." "Well, she was a little weird," Gabby says, "and I don't think we'll get stuck in her class again anyway. Besides I think the story is so cool, I would love to know more about the legend. When we get back to the parking lot at the customs office we can go in and ask if there's a place we might find information about the hut?" Jack can see the excitement in the girls' eyes. "You know," Jack says, "why don't we finish the tour later and head back now so you two can get started on the research?" "Would you mind?" Gabby asks. "No, not at all," Jack said with a smile. "We have the entire summer to see the island. Also, I have a surprise for you two." "Cool!" Susan says. Jack continues, "I put both of you on the insurance for the truck, which means you can drive it and have transportation while you're here. Kind of a present from me. But be careful running around here, people don't drive like they do in the states. They'll run over you if you're not careful."

Jack parks in front of the customs office and hands Gabby the keys. "You know this is a straight stick, do you know how to drive one?" "I think we'll be alright," Gabby answers. "Daddy showed me how to drive our five-speed at home." "How about you Susan?" Jack asks. "Well," Susan answers, "I've never driven one before, but how hard could it be?" Jack continues, "Gabby, you might take her to a secluded place and let her try working the clutch and gears. By the way did you two bring your driver's licenses?" Gabby answers, "We've got them, want to see?" "No," Jack says, "I don't need to see, just don't forget them when you go out. There's a map of the island in the glove box if you need it. You should have enough gas, but if not the map will show you where to fill up. I'm heading back to the boat." Then he adds, "Here, take one of the radios with you and when you get ready for me to pick you up at the dock, give me a call on channel sixty-nine and I'll run the dink over." "That will work," Gabby says as Jack walks down to the dock to dinghy out to Gypsy Wind. Susan looks at Gabby and says, "This is going to be great, having our own truck!" "I know!" Gabby replies. "Let's go in the customs office and get started." "Cool," Susan says, "Totally cool!"

Chapter

3

Gabby and Susan walk into the customs office. The office building is one of only three buildings on the island that has two stories. They look around at the seating area, which is rather small compared to most they are familiar with in the states. The area looks as if time has stood still from the sixties. A chrome-framed sofa and chairs with green plastic covers sit to the left of the entrance.

A table is located between the two chairs, holding a magazine or two. The floor is white tile which has been waxed to a high gloss finish. The office seems deserted. Just then, a customs officer walks past the doorway located behind the counter leading to offices in the back and sees the girls at the counter. The customs officer is a dark-skinned lady in her mid-thirties who has lived on the island all her life. She completed her schooling on Bonaire and attended college in Venezuela. Many of the families with college age children send them to Venezuela to complete their schooling. However, most of them never return to the island life. Instead they find jobs in Venezuela, and only return to Bonaire to visit family and friends from time to time. Margo Warzes is different, in that she was able to land the customs job (which required a college education). Having a job with the customs office is regarded as very prestigious and one of the best jobs on the island due to the good pay and steady work, not to mention the power that comes with the position. "Hello, my name is Customs Officer Margo Warzes, may I help you?" "Yes, thank you," Gabby speaks up. "We hope you might be able to help us with information regarding a little research we're doing."

# BONAIRE CUSTOMS

**CUSTOMS OFFICER
MARGO WARZES**

"What kind of research?" the officer asks. "Well, my friend and I are interested in any information, or places that might have information, regarding the Witch's Hut on the north end of the island." By the look on her face, Officer Warzes is obviously shocked at the question. Gabby and Susan notice this immediately. "Why in the world would you two lovely young ladies want information on such an evil place?" Officer Warzes asks. "Well," Gabby says, "Susan and I are down here for the summer, sailing with my grandfather. You might know his boat, Gypsy Wind. Anyway, Susan and I have been studying the occult at school and we would like to do a paper on the Witch's Hut. Do you know anywhere we might be able to find information?" The Officer looks at the girls and asks, "What did you say your names are?" "I'm sorry," Gabby says. "My name is Gabriella Varde, this is Susan Maddox, and my grandfather is Jack Elder." "Well Gabriella and Susan," Officer Warzes replies, "there might be a place you can find information about the witch's hut, but I would suggest you find something else to write about." Gabby and Susan look at each other then back at Officer Warzes, waiting for her answer. "I was once young and curious myself," Officer Warzes says. "But understand, there is evil in those charred walls. I would suggest you stay as far away from there as you can. But if I were looking for information about the hut, I would start at the Historical Center over by the bank building. They might have some information for you there." "Just where is the bank building?" Gabby asks. "Right down the street," Officer Warzes says, as she points back toward town. "The bank building is on the right, just beyond the one-way entrance to the main street that runs through town. You can't miss it." "Thank you so much," Gabby says, as the girls turn and walk out. Susan thinks for a moment then says, "Gabby, why don't we walk down there? It can't be very far." "Sounds like a good idea to me," Gabby agrees. "We'll leave the truck here in the parking lot." Officer Warzes watches the girls leave, then turns to see her co-worker emerging from the back area. She makes eye contact with him and shakes her head saying, "Kids, that's all, just kids. Let's get back to work, we've got another ship due tonight."

## Chapter 4

Jack is on the deck of Gypsy Wind, putting a coat of varnish on a teak deck rail just in front of the main mast on the port side of his boat. Anchored off his port is a sweet little thirty-seven foot sloop called Wanderlust, owned by Lisa Wilkerson. Lisa and her husband moved to the island some three years earlier and, for whatever reason, divorced shortly after arriving. Lisa got the boat in the divorce and also kept the dream, remaining on the island to run her own charter boat business.

She and Jack hit it off immediately after running into each other at the pier bar, one evening shortly after Jack arrived on the island. Once they learned they were anchored next to each other in the harbor, the friendship grew quickly. Lisa was around forty-five years of age, five feet, six-inches tall, with long gray hair and a good figure. The sun had taken its toll over the years and she looked to be fifty-five or better, with skin like leather. Lisa could talk for hours on just about any subject that came up, which made for enjoyable evening conversations at sunset. She was a pure joy to sit and pass the time with, and she and Jack would sometimes talk late into the night.

Jack looks to port and notices Lisa on deck and waves. "How's it going this morning?" he calls across the water. Lisa returns the wave and says, "Super, did your granddaughter make it in yesterday?" "Yes, they're somewhere on the island now," Jack replies.

**LISA**

"Why don't you bring them to the bar tonight for sunset, I would like to meet them," Lisa says. "Sounds like a great idea, we'll be there," Jack replies, then he goes back to work. Gabby and Susan walk to the front door of the Historical Center. The door squeaks as it opens and they walk in. It looks more like a library than anything else.

Gabby slowly scans the room. It smells of old books and papers, which have an odor of mildew about them. She walks to the desk where she finds a dome shaped silver bell. She pushes the button on top, the bell rings, and a lady steps out from behind a row of books in the back. The lady is in her mid-sixties, with gray hair, and she speaks with an accent that Susan and Gabby can't place. It's more than likely a mixture of local dialect with a little Dutch and Spanish mixed all together. They have a hard time understanding the old woman at first. "Hello," the old woman says. "Hello," Susan responds. "Can I help you?" the woman asks. "Yes, I hope so," Susan replies. "We hope you might have some information regarding the Witch's Hut, something about the history and such." The old woman has a puzzled look on her face then says, "That's something I haven't been asked about in a long time. You ladies come with me." The old woman leads

Gabby and Susan to the back of the building. They can tell this area of the library has not seen many people in quite some time. Upon reaching the back, the girls find themselves in front of a wall of wooden drawers which reach to the twelve foot ceiling. The cabinets are dusty and look to be very old. They are beautifully crafted, with carvings decorating the outer edge of the wall unit. The old woman pulls a drawer open and takes out what seems to be a manuscript about as thick as a standard dictionary. She then lays it carefully on the table. "First, you two need to bring this out to the front if you would like to go through it, and you must wear gloves at all times. I have two pair up front that you can use. If you would like to have a copy made it will cost two dollars U.S. per page." "Why so much?" Gabby asks. The old women replies, "Copy machines and toner are very expensive on a small island, not to mention the paper, which has to be imported as well. Also, as you can see, it's written in Spanish and I don't have time to translate." "That won't be necessary, we understand the language quite well," Susan replies. Gabby asks, "Is this all you have regarding the subject?" "Yes dear, I'm afraid so," the old woman replies, "and you're not going to find much in there either. But it should get you started. It is from the same time frame as the tale of the tragedy. As I recall, there might be something that references the death of the young girl and the names of the family members. I think it was in Rincon. But it's been a long time since I've seen the manuscript." The woman looks at Susan and Gabby then says, "There's not much told about the old house up there. Most people think of it as bad luck to even mention the old home. If I were you, I would look for something else to study, nothing but bad things happen to those who enter that old house." "Thank you," Gabby says, as the girls sit down to look through the book.

Gabby opens what at first glance looks like a manuscript, but finds what seems to be a diary of some sort, written by a local priest in the late 1800's through the mid-1900's. The diary has monthly entries regarding the business of the church, information spanning fifty years - business transactions, family names of children born, family members who passed away. "Look Susan, here's an entry about the Treaty of Paris and when the Dutch took over the island." "Gabby, check this out, slavery was abolished in 1863," Susan stated, "This is cool. There's all kinds of stuff here. They had a weeklong festival in the towns of Kralendijk and Rincon." "Ok Susan," Gabby breaks in, "what we need to find is anything about the young girl's death, sometime in the early to mid-twenties."

Gabby and Susan carefully look over every page for anything that might give them a clue. Two hours pass before Gabby finally says "Here's something about a child being kidnapped and the death of her mother." Gabby and Susan look at each other as if they had found a $100 dollar bill. "That's it Gabby, that's the girl!" Susan exclaimed excitedly. "I think you're right," Gabby replied, "it's got to be the little girl." "Does it give a name?" Susan asks. "Yes, the name is Andrea!" Gabby excitedly replies. "Translate it Gabby," Susan asks. "I'll try," Gabby says, "but the writing is hard to read. Date, the fourth day of June, nineteen-fifteen, day of the Festival of Dia Di, Rincon. The child of Andrea Reina and Carlos Reina was kidnapped from her home by pirates, identities unknown at this time. Andrea Reina was killed during the assault and is survived by her husband, Carlos Reina, and great-grandmother Shania Salvador of Rincon. Susan, that looks like all there is." "Well, that's not much, but it verifies that the story your granddaddy told us is true, or at least the part about the abduction and murder. I don't know about all that voodoo stuff though." "Ya," Gabby agrees, "we need to find out if there are any descendents of the great-grandmother. We need to go to Rincon!"

It is seven o'clock in the evening and Jack pulls away from Gypsy Wind in the dink. He is heading for the dock and the nightly gathering of cruisers having a drink while watching the celebrated sunset. Jack has not seen Gabby or Susan all day, so he expects he'll run into them on the dock. Also, he promised Lisa he would introduce her to the girls.

As Jack climbs onto the dock, he sees Lisa sitting at a table with two strangers he has not seen before. He realizes they must be new customers. Lisa sees him and waves. Jack nods to her, then finds just the right table. He settles down and starts looking out for Gabby and Susan when his radio sounds off. "Gypsy Wind, come in." Jack pushes the button, "This is Gypsy Wind, go ahead." "Granddaddy, could you come pick us up? We're at the dock." "Sure sweetheart, but first why don't you two walk down the dock to the bar for a coke and some munchies with me?" "You're at the dock already?" Gabby asks. "I'm here," Jack replies.

Gabby and Susan spot Jack and head for the table. Pulling up chairs, the girls start filling Jack in on all they have done regarding their research.

Lisa completes her business with the couple and

heads over to Jack's table. "Hi Jack, how about introducing your friends?" "Hi Lisa, have a seat," Jack says. "Lisa, I would like to introduce my granddaughter, Gabriella Varde, and her very good friend Susan Maddox. Girls, this is Lisa Wilkerson. She's anchored next to us on Wanderlust, and runs a charter service here on the island." Gabby and Susan respond simultaneously saying, "Glad to meet you Miss Wilkerson." Lisa says, "Please, not so formal! Call me Lisa."

"How have you two been enjoying the island so far?" Lisa asks. "Just fine," Gabby replies. "Susan and I have been doing a little research on the old Witch's Hut." Lisa looks shocked, which is a look Gabby and Susan are starting to get used to. "What in the world would you want to research that old place for?" Lisa asks. "Well," Gabby replies, "Susan and I just completed a paper for school on the subject of voodoo. After hearing the story from Granddaddy we just couldn't help ourselves. We have to know more." "Very interesting," Lisa says. "What have you found out so far?" Gabby continues, "We found out that the story is true about the kidnapping of the little girl and the death of her mother. The girl's name that Granddaddy told us, that was correct as well. They have or had family over in Rincon. We hope to go over there tomorrow and see if we can find anyone left that might be able to give us some more background on the story." Jack butts in, "Lisa I haven't been over there yet, do you think the girls will be ok on their own in Rincon?" "Yeah they will be fine," Lisa answers. "Not much going on around here except petty theft, that's about all. You girls make sure you don't leave anything in the truck or it will be gone." Susan shakes her head, "We've been told that more than once already."

Gabby looks at Susan, then at Jack. "Granddaddy, would you mind if Susan and I head back to the boat? We want to take a swim and have a shower using your new shower on the deck." Jack leans over and gives Gabby a big hug then says, "Sure sweetheart, take the dink. I'll get Lisa to drop me off when she heads back to Wanderlust." "Thanks," Gabby says as she and Susan stand up. "It was very nice to meet you Ms. Wilkerson, I mean Lisa. We hope to see you later." Lisa replies, "Yes I'm sure we'll see a lot of each other before the summer ends."

After the girls have left, Lisa says, "Jack, they seem like two very independent young ladies." Jack smiles then replies, "Thanks. They are as intelligent as they are independent. I never know what's going to come out of their mouths. They sure keep me on my toes."

"I'm sure they will do well once they get out on their own someday," Lisa agrees. Lisa and Jack raise their glasses, as if toasting to the future success of the girls.

The evening sky is unveiling its nightly palette of purples and reds for the anxious cruisers gathered at the bar for the evening show. The colors seem to be brushed across the horizon. Meanwhile, Gabby and Susan make their way back to Gypsy Wind to cool off and plan the next day's adventure.

Sitting on the deck of Gypsy Wind after a relaxing swim and solar shower, the girls talk.

"Look Susan, that looks like a freighter way off on the horizon heading this way. That must be where those tugboats were heading a while ago, to meet it. I wonder what's down on the other end of the island where it's headed? You know, I think I read somewhere that it's a fuel storage facility or something like that. It would make sense having it on the far end of the island, away from town. I'll bet that's a fuel tanker from Venezuela."

"You know, I really do like this place, "Susan says. "I wonder how long the music will play at the bar tonight? It sure is cool sitting here listening to the island sounds." The sun has already slipped behind Klein Bonaire, highlighting the small growth on the island. The sky reminds Gabby of the old saying her Granddaddy loves to recite. She thinks to herself, "Red sky at night, sailors delight." As Gypsy Wind sits at anchor, Susan and Gabby can smell different fragrances drifting across the water from the restaurants located next to the pier.

"I don't know about you Gabby but I'm tired. Why don't we turn in?" Gabby agrees. "I could use a little sleep as well. Tomorrow is going to be a busy day!"

Later in the evening, Jack and Lisa motor alongside Gypsy Wind. Jack says, "It looks like the girls didn't wait up for old Granddad." "Well," Lisa replies, "Do you blame them? I'm sure it must have taken a lot out of them chasing witches and such all day." Jack looks back at Lisa and smiles. "Thanks for the ride. I'll see you tomorrow." "Sounds like a plan to me," Lisa replies as she pulls away from Gypsy Wind. Jack makes a final check of the boat before turning in. This has become his nightly ritual. Jack shakes his head as he finds the dinghy unlocked. He pulls it along side and jumps down and sets the lock in place. "Now it's my turn for bed," he thinks to himself as he heads down the aft companionway to the master cabin. Meanwhile, Susan and Gabby are fast asleep in the vee-berth as Gypsy Wind swings at anchor in the light breezes. The music continues to drift from the dock as the midnight hour approaches.

## Chapter 5

That same evening, far out to sea, an oil tanker from a Venezuelan port lumbers along through moderate winds and five foot swells, heading for Bonaire. The tanker, at 600 tons and 265 feet in length, is the Venezuelan Crescent. The ship is fully loaded with goods that help sustain the island. The old tanker has been in service for many years. The company that owns the Venezuelan Crescent has neglected the old ship over her years of service, opting instead, out of greed, to divert the money required to maintain the old tanker elsewhere. The captain had, on many occasions, put into a nearby port rather than chance high seas during bad weather, due to the tankers condition.

Standing on the bridge while smoking a pipe, the captain is a striking figure. He has spent most his life on the sea, first with his father as a fisherman and then later working his way up to captain with ship line after ship line. He has been with the Crescent ship line for the past twenty years with over a hundred-thousand miles logged. Captain Salvador is looking forward to retirement, which is only one year away. Every trip to Bonaire these days is profitable for the old captain, and not only because of his yearly salary.

"Captain, we are in sight of Bonaire and at the outer marker may I call in?" Captain Salvador turns and says with a stern voice, "Call." The crewmember calls in. "BOPEC station, this is the tanker Venezuelan

Crescent, requesting permission to enter and requesting docking tenders." A voice blasts through the speaker, "Venezuelan Crescent, tenders will tie off at marker ZX454. over." "Affirmative, Venezuelan Crescent, out." "Captain, we have to make for marker 454." "Very well, take the helm until the pilot master boards. I'll be in my cabin." Captain Salvador turns and heads down the ladder to his cabin. While preparing the ship's documentation for customs, he leans back into his chair and his mind wanders into the past to the first time he made this trip. "How young and inexperienced I was in those days," he thinks. "Many years and many miles I've traveled and with nothing to show for it except a broken home and a son who hardly knows who I am. The old saying is true, the sea allows no other mistress." The Captain shakes his head as he places the paper work into a large envelope and seals it.

On Bonaire, the BOPEC station contacts the town pier, which in turn dispatches two tenders from the dock. The pilot master is aboard one of the tenders. He will take control of the ship while docking is underway. Under his watchful eye, tugs will assist in the control of the tanker while bringing it alongside the unloading dock at BOPEC station. There, the valuable cargo will be offloaded.

In town at the customs office, Warzes gets in her van with the proper paperwork and heads for the BOPEC station, to clear the tanker into port. One of the jobs of the customs office is to clear the ship's cargo before offloading can commence. The tanker is carrying more than just fuel. Medical products must be offloaded and delivered to the local hospital on the island.

The customs officer will take possession of some of the more important medical supplies and clear them through customs personally before handing them over to the hospital. Other supplies will move through the clearing process much more slowly due to their lesser level of importance.

**CAPTAIN SALVADOR**

The Venezuelan Crescent inches closer to the docks at BOPEC, with the assistance of the tugboats. Lines are secured and Officer Warzes boards the ship, heading for the captain's cabin. She knocks on the cabin door and Captain Salvador pulls it open to greet her. "Hello," the captain says in greeting. "Please come in, we have much to talk about." "Thank you Captain," Officer Warzes answers, "I hope your crossing was uneventful." Captain Salvador replies, "Very uneventful, thank you."

"Captain, did you bring the medical supplies?" Officer Warzes asks. Captain Salvador leans back into his chair and smiles. "I have the supplies, and I think you'll be very pleased indeed. Did you bring the money?" Officer Warzes replies, "I did."

Captain Salvador stands up and says, "Well, let's get to it." They leave the cabin and head up on deck. Captain Salvador motions to one of the crew members. "Seaman open deck container number 636HH and unload the white packages with the red medical cross on the side. There should be two of them. I want you to deliver them to my quarters." The seaman turns with a snap and heads for the container.

Captain Salvador and Officer Warzes make their way back to the Captain's quarters and the seaman delivers the packages as ordered. He places the boxes on the captain's bed and promptly leaves the cabin, closing the door behind him. "Let's take a look and see what we have here," the captain says.

Captain Salvador removes several bags of what seem to be medication of some kind before pulling two boxes out and handing them to Officer Warzes. She opens the first box to find one engraved plate, which looks to be a duplicate of a U.S. twenty dollar bill. Officer Warzes hands an envelope over to the captain with a smile and say's, "Looks good captain. I think this concludes our business." The captain smiles as he looks into the envelope then says, "Yes, our business here is done. I'll have a crewmember carry the rest of the supplies down to your vehicle."

Officer Warzes walks down the gangway and leaves the ship, heading for her van with the seaman in tow. With the boxes loaded in the van, the seaman nods his head and returns to the ship. "I think I'll run it over now and drop off the medical supplies later," Officer Warzes thinks to herself.

## Chapter 6

It is six-thirty in the morning and Gypsy Wind is rocking from side-to-side as a wake moves across the anchorage from seaward. Fishermen in their open boats disturb the flat calm water as they head out for a day of fishing. Later in the evening, their catch of the day will be available at the open air market along the water front. Many of the local restaurants will find their "seafood catch of the day" for their daily menu, once the fishermen have returned. Even now, in this day and time, some islanders still rely on the sea for a living.

The gentle rocking of the boat has brought Gabby out of her deep sleep. As she opens her eyes she sees the water's reflection coming through the porthole, dancing throughout the v-berth. As it dances, the light captivates the eye much like gazing into a fireplace, as flames dart in and out of the embers.

Gabby starts mentally planning her day of research, and then she hears Susan start to move around on the upper bunk. "Susan, are you awake?" Gabby asks. "Yes," comes the sleepy answer, "how about you?" Gabby starts to laugh and says, "No I'm still asleep." Susan starts to laugh as well. "Let's get up and find something to eat," Gabby suggests. "Ok," Susan replies. The girls get up and whip up a quick breakfast of toast and jelly. Gabby reaches over and flips the coffee on to brew for Jack, then remembers they are not on shore power and the coffee pot pulls a lot of power. She thinks for a moment then turns the coffee pot off and says out loud, "You know, I think I'd better let Granddaddy turn his coffee on. I don't know how long he's going to sleep, and there's no need running the coffee maker if we don't have to." Although Gypsy Wind has a wind generator as well as solar panels, power is always a concern on a sail boat while at anchor. Jack even runs the engine every other day for thirty minutes, to help the recharging process.

After breakfast, Gabby and Susan gather their things for their day in Rincon. Gabby writes Jack a note, telling him where they plan to go.

"Granddaddy, I hope you don't mind, but Susan and I want to get an early start before it gets too hot. I have the radio with me, so if you need to call I'll have it on. We'll leave the dink at the dock, but we'll lock it up. Remember to call us if you want us to come back so you can get the dink to motor around with. Love, Gabby and Susan." Gabby looks at Susan and says, "That should do it. Let's go." The girls climb down into the dink. Susan pulls the rope and the outboard comes to life, as they immediately start to move forward and head to the dock.

At the truck, Gabby starts the engine and slips the transmission into first gear. The two wanderers are off down the road. Before they know it, they are at a four-way junction. The sign indicates that Rincon is straight ahead. Pulling away from the stop sign, Susan laughs, "Gabby look!" "What?" Gabby asks. Susan points and says, "Lisa owns a filling station." "What in the world are you talking about?" Gabby says. The filling station is named Lisa Gas. "The lady that your grandfather introduced us to last night was named Lisa, wasn't she?" Gabby thinks for a second then says, "Yes." "Well?" Susan persists. "Well what?" Gabby asks again. "Do you think she owns it?" Gabby laughs, "I don't think so, but the next time you see her, why don't you ask." "I think I will," Susan says, "We might be able to get free gas." Susan smiles as the truck heads down the road to Rincon.

Once in Rincon, the girls pull off the road and scan the area, wondering what to do next. "Well," Gabby says, "what do you think?" Susan ponders the question and replies, "I think we should find the local church or graveyard." "Good thinking," Gabby says as she re-starts the truck, then they drive around looking for one or the other. After about ten minutes, Gabby spots a cemetery. The cemetery is located right in the middle of a row of homes on a side street. She can tell the cemetery plots have been taken care of. The old graveyard has a wall that reaches completely around it. The walls are made of what looks to be coral and it is painted a white that is so bright it hurts the eyes to look at it. Gabby can feel the roughness under her hand as she pulls the old wrought-iron gate open. The elements have taken their toll on the metal gate over the years, and rust has taken over. As the girls walk around the old (and in some cases damaged) headstones, they find nothing that relates to the young girl's name that they had gotten from the manuscript in the library. "Well, I don't know which way to go from here," Gabby says. She raises her head and sees a church steeple on the next street over, towering above the rooftops. "Susan look, a steeple!" Gabby is pointing over the houses. "Cool, I see it, let's check it out," Susan says. They return to the truck and drive around the block to the church. The church is plain and unassuming, and has obviously been standing for many years. The girls pull the truck alongside the road and park in the white sand and gravel that covers the roadside. Closing the truck door, Gabby hesitates before crossing the street to take in the sight. Her mind races back in time and she can almost visualize the local people of the town walking down the roadside for their Sunday mass, the priest on the top step greeting everyone with open arms. "Gabby, let's go!" Susan's words return her to the present and the two girls cross the street. The church is unlocked and they walk in. Susan says, "Gabby, I'm not so sure this is a good idea." "Oh quit whining," Gabby says. It seems that the girls are the only two in the whole church. Gabby can't help but admire the interior. At first glance, the inside is as plain as the outside. Her eyes make a closer inspection of the interior and discover beautifully crafted pews with hand carvings on each end, no doubt carved by some local artist in the congregation. The walls are painted white which accents the dark wood loft, visible from her vantage point below. Wooden stairs in the corners up front lead upstairs.

    A man in work pants and an old tattered shirt walks in the door behind them and ask in Spanish if he can help them. Gabby replies in Spanish saying, "Yes please." The light is breaking through the front door where the man is standing, making it hard for the girls to see him clearly due to the glare. As Gabby moves closer, she realizes a white collar is around his neck. She says, "We are so sorry to intrude Father, my name is Gabriella Varde and this is Susan Maddox. We are doing some research regarding a family that once lived in Rincon many years ago." "Varde, that's Latin, is it not?" the priest asks. Gabby answers, "Yes sir, my father is Chilean."

CHURCH

"Who are you looking for? Maybe I can be of some help." Gabby takes a paper from her bag and hands it to the priest. Written on the paper are the names of Andrea and Carlos Renia. The priest ponders the names, thinking out loud. Gabby hesitates to mention the Witch's Hut when the priest looks at the girls and says, "I think I know these names. May I ask why you wish to speak to them?" Gabby thinks for a moment, and then answers the priest. "Susan and I are interested in the story of the couple and the events surrounding the death of the young girl named Andrea. We mean no disrespect to the surviving family members, but we think the story would be something that might be shared with others in our school class back in the states." The priest asks the girls to follow him to his office. Entering the office, Gabby scans the room and notices the room has large windows which are wide open. The little church more than likely has no air conditioning. The priest asks them to sit down while he pulls the information from his files. Gabby, still looking the room over, sees an adjoining room with the door half open. Inside she can see modest furniture with a cross over the bed. She realizes that this place is the priest's home, as well as his parish. "It looks like the surviving members of the Renia family no longer live on the island." Gabby and Susan look at each other with disappointment in their eyes. The priest looks over at Gabby and says, "But I think there might be some descendants of Andrea's family. Her maiden name was Andrea Cortes, and my records indicate we have a family with that last name here, but an address is not available." Gabby asks if any first names are available.

The Priest obliges with the name of Manny, which is short for Manuel. The girls thank him and the priest walks them back to the front doors and bids them farewell. The entire conversation has taken place in Spanish, and after returning to the truck Susan says, "Wow Gabby, you did great. It felt good holding our own completely in the language." "Yeah, we did well," Gabby replies. "Now, let's regroup and figure out our next move." Gabby and Susan head back to Kralendijk, and then to the boat for a late lunch. They need some time to make notes and plans for their next day of detective work.

Jack is sitting in the heat of the day, reading to pass the time. Any boat repairs and maintenance must be done in the morning or the late afternoon, due to the intense heat. Today is the day he will start the engine, to help recharge the batteries. Jack notices his fuel is nearing the half empty mark and realizes he needs to start thinking about refueling at some point. He remembers that Lisa told him she was planning to head over to Venezuela where fuel was considerably more affordable per gallon. "Maybe I could follow her over with the girls," Jack thinks.

He hears an outboard coming alongside. "It's the girls," he says to himself as he climbs out of his beanbag chair to help them tie up and come aboard. "Did you girls have fun today?" Jack asks. "We had a great day Granddaddy, and we found out some more about the family. We are heading back over to Rincon tomorrow to see if we can find some of the ancestors. Meanwhile let's see what's in here for lunch!"

## Chapter 7

It is 11:00 p.m. and a light comes on in the still of the night. A young man, dressed in gray work pants, a t-shirt, and tennis shoes, walks to a table and starts cutting large sheets of paper. A little later he hears a four-wheeler pull up outside, and an older man named Wonka walks in. "Hi Moog," Wonka says. "Hola," Moog replies, "did the plates get here?" "Si," Wonka answers, "these are the best ones yet!"

# MOOG

Wonka walks over and surveys the new plates, running his hands across them. "Very nice. But before we set them, we have to get rid of the money we have. How much longer will it take for you to get everything cut and ready to go?" Moog thinks. "I should be done by tomorrow night, if this ink will dry. I told you it would be too humid in a cave." "Well," Wonka replies, "do the best you can. I'll get in touch with our contact tomorrow and tell them we'll be ready in a day or so." Moog bids Wonka goodbye and gets back to cutting the counterfeit $100 dollar bills. Moog is small of build, in his early twenties. He is considered not very bright by many of the local islanders who know him. Moog dropped out of high school before graduating, due to behavioral problems as well as academic concerns. Now, like many underachievers, he has been manipulated into illegal endeavors which could land him in jail some day.

 Wonka is well known by the locals. He is in his late fifties, and is short, with a stocky build. He has lived alone for ten years, ever since his wife left the island and never returned. He works at the fuel storage facility BOPEC, at the north end of the island, as a crane operator. He has lived most of his life on the island and, as locals go, has a rather well-to-do life.

Wonka turns and heads back out the curtain covering the cave opening, making sure to close it behind him. Moog hears the four-wheeler start as Wonka makes his its way down the dirt trail to the coast road.

WONKA

Inside the cave on the table is a large stack of paper. Each sheet contains thirty individually printed $100 dollar bills, the ink barely dry.

It is the afternoon of the next day when Wonka's cell phone rings. "Look Wonka, the pickup is set for tomorrow night." "I don't think we will be ready by then," Wonka replies, "we had problems with this batch of ink, and it's too damp."

"That's tough, but we have no choice. That's the way it has to be. They're on the way now and I, for one, don't want to have to tell them they wasted a trip! Do you? So it's tomorrow night, like it or not! Now listen to what I'm saying Wonka. Package up the bills in water proof bags and just be ready to go! Understand?" Wonka nods his head as if his boss on the other end of the phone can see him. "And make sure you burn any bills that are unusable. I don't want any trace of those bills laying around for someone to find. Wonka, do you understand me?" "Si," Wonka says, "I understand. I'll be ready." His boss continues,

"The boat will come ashore at 2:15 a.m., at the same location as always. Have the signals ready and the stuff packed and ready to hand over. If the signals are not lit, they will not come ashore. Collect the $100,000.00 dollars and get out of there before someone sees you. We'll meet at the office. Do you understand?" "I understand," Wonka reassures his boss once again.

    Miles offshore, a sailboat under power, showing no sails or running lights, heads for Bonaire with a three-man crew aboard. The three have a deadline to make which could make all three quite wealthy if they complete their mission undetected. The trio are killers and drug runners, and could be considered modern day pirates. With a little luck they should make their destination with time to spare, holding off the coast, out of sight of land, until the right moment for the pickup.

# Chapter 8

It is the next morning and the girls are planning another day looking for descendents of Andrea.

Jack is getting Gypsy Wind ready for the crossing to Venezuela and the port of Puerto La Cruz. Gabby and Susan are told to be back from their adventure by 7:00 p.m., for dinner and the departure. They are making the crossing with Lisa. They'll follow her to Puerto Viejo Marina to fill up with fuel.

Gabby and Susan are off again to Rincon but Gabby decides to go a different route this time. "Gabby, where are you going," Susan asks with a puzzled look on her face. "I'm going to try another way today. I think we went a long way out of the way yesterday." Gabby is following the same road Jack had taken them on when they were sightseeing up on the north end of the island, the day they were first introduced to the Witch's Hut.

Winding around the different turns, Gabby finds herself driving down a steep hill heading toward the ocean, then the road makes a sharp turn to the right. Susan says, "Stop here for a minute, the yellow rock over there says Oil Slick Leap. What a name for a dive site. It's probably full of oil drums." "Don't be silly," Gabby says, "That is a rather odd name though." Gabby pulls onto the road again and heads north. She is constantly dodging lizards, running for their life from one side of the road to the other. Susan complains, "These things act like they're playing some kind of death game, running back and forth across the road" "Yeah, I think you're right," Gabby says, "and I think from the looks of it some of them didn't play the game too well." They both laugh as they dodge another reptile.

Gabby slows and pulls off the road at a dive site marked with a yellow rock, with the name Weber's Joy written on it. Susan looks at Gabby as they both get out of the truck and turn from the sand spit which marks the entrance to the dive site. They look across the road at the Witch's Hut, standing alone with the hills, caves, and underbrush as its backdrop.

"Let's check this place out Susan," Gabby says. Susan looks at Gabby and says, "Why not?" The two walk to the front door and enter the dwelling. In the front room to the left of the door is what seems to have been a fireplace. Gabby thinks it might have been the place the meals were cooked because it's mounted up off the floor rather than on the floor like a real fireplace would be. Anyway, who would need a fireplace on a desert island? They move into the back rooms which could have been bedrooms. The little home is small, but in its day it was very adequate for life on the small island. As they leave the house, Gabby notices the large window to the right of the door, overlooking the water. Graffiti is written on almost every wall, indicating that people had been in the house, dismissing the tale that no one ever entered it due to bad luck. "What a pity," she thinks to herself shaking her head, "such a lovely home once upon a time." The girls get back in the truck and make their way down the road. Before taking the right turn east, which leads to Rincon and inland from the sea, they pull off the road once again. "It looks like this might be a picnic area," Susan says. "Look, there is a cover over the concrete table." To the left is what appears to be a small boat ramp and just beyond that are three rowboats. The boats look as though they have not been used for years and they have fallen into disrepair.

Gabby and Susan look to the right and see the main gate to the fuel storage facility, which is just beyond the turn in the road. After a few minutes the girls continue on.

Once in Rincon, they set to work looking for clues that might lead them somehow to a name or location. Gabby spots a telephone company and thinks, "What if they're listed?" She pulls off the road in front of the door. "Susan, lets go in and see if they have a phonebook of some type." "Gabby you don't really think it's going to be that easy do you?" Gabby replies, "Well no, but I don't know what else to do." Susan agrees and they head into the building where they find a nice gentleman who is eager to help them locate the address they need. In record time he returns with the information, as well as directions. "I don't believe it," Gabby says with surprise in her voice. Susan is even more shocked. Gabby and Susan thank the man and head down the road, following the directions given to them. After turning off the main road of Kaya

Encarvacion B. Sint Jago, they take the next left onto Kaya Trintaria, which is very close to the church they had visited the day before.

Once on Kaya Trintaria, they take another left onto Kaya Magdalena. They spot the house at the same time, on the right-hand side of the street. "There it is," Susan points. "I see it," Gabby replies. She pulls over, half on the street and half on the dirt shoulder of the road.

They walk up to the front door which is standing wide open. Gabby's eyes scan the area looking for someone, but she only sees chickens walking around the front porch. They are sitting on the rusted old swing that's hanging from the ceiling of the porch as well. She leans in through the door, only sticking her head in half way. Raising her voice, she calls, "Hello is anyone here?"

An older lady comes from the back of the house and answers, "Yes can I help you?" Gabby replies, "Yes please. I'm looking for a family or family member with the last name of Cortes. Do I have the right place?" "Yes dear, that is my last name. May I help you?" Gabby and Susan look at each other and grin. "Hello," Gabby says, and then she introduces Susan and herself to the lady. "Mrs. Cortes, Susan and I have been doing some research regarding a possible family descendant of yours by the name of Andrea Renia." The lady invites Gabby and Susan to come in and have a seat. She introduces herself as Mrs. Sabrina Cortes, and she is visibly taken aback by the statement she has just received from Gabby. Mrs. Cortes looks at the two girls and says, "I have not heard that name in thirty years. I'm sorry if I look surprised. Why in the world would you be interested in Andrea, for heaven's sake?" Gabby relates the research she and Susan are doing, then asks if they would be imposing to ask a few questions. Mrs. Cortes agrees but says, "Why don't you two come out back, where we can sit? I'm sure it will be much cooler there than here in the house. Would you like some lemonade?" The girls are more than happy to say yes, and the three of them sit under the shade tree, drinks in hand, enjoying the slight breeze blowing through the back yard. The yard is well kept, with little or no grass. A small garden is off to the side of the house and a goat, presumably for milk, is tied to a tree. The family is as self-sufficient as possible on the small island, where everything can cost double due to the import tax.

    Gabby sits on a metal glider with Mrs. Cortes, while Susan sits across from them in a metal rocking chair of the same style. Gabby asks, "Mrs. Cortes, can you tell us if the story told of Andrea's death is true?"

"Well dear, I was told the story as a child many years ago, and it was relayed to me the same way as you understand it now. The husband Carlos never came back to the island as far as I know, and the baby girl was never found. Gabby asks about the grandmother. "Yes," Mrs. Cortes says, "The grandmother did indeed exist as well. Mama Shania was what everyone called her. She put a spell on the house and whoever killed Andrea. That's the way the story has always been told to me and the other kids." Gabby has one more question to ask. "Mrs. Cortes, I don't suppose you have any photos of the grandmother, the child or Andrea and her husband?" "Well dear, I think so, but I'll have to try and find them for you. Can you come back tomorrow?" Gabby frowns. "I don't think so, my grandfather is heading over to Venezuela for fuel and I'm not sure when we will get back. We will be on the island for the whole summer though. Could we come back sometime next week? I'm sure we'll be back by then." "Of course, dear." Mrs. Cortes replies. "Oh, by the way, the priest told us that there was someone named Manny Cortes, does he live here too?" "Of course dear, that is my older son. But he has been gone from the island for about five years. He lives in your country, in New York City." Gabby and Susan thank Mrs. Cortes and help her with the drink glasses and tray. The girls walk back to the truck in disbelief that they found the family so easily. "Large families on small islands are easy to find," Gabby thinks to herself.

## Chapter 9

Jack has Gypsy Wind as ready as she is going to be for the crossing ahead. He has pulled the dink on board and lashed it to the forward deck. Some wind is finding its way under the dink and into the interior of the boat, which will help come afternoon as the day heats up. The time is 11:30 p.m., which Jack likes to call 2330 hours. Lisa would have liked to pull anchor much earlier, but was unable to do so due to her passengers' schedule. The two passengers are customers who needed a ride to Curacao, and that means good money for her.

Lisa unties from the buoy and slowly drifts away from the anchorage, paying careful attention to the other boats around her. Jack plans to follow her to Curacao, and then to Puerto La Cruz for fuel. Susan is on board Lisa's boat, acting as crew for the crossing, while Gabby is with Jack. "Gabby, let's pull the anchor and get out of here," Jack says. Gabby thinks for a moment then says, "Granddaddy we're tied off to the buoy, the anchor is onboard." "I know," Jack laughs, "it's just a figure of speech. Let's get out of here." Gabby unties Gypsy Wind, and secures the line on the deck.

The plan is to head up the coast to the north end of the island, then turn slightly northwest toward Curacao.

Lisa and Jack decided to make a night departure due to the ever-changing weather window. Conditions look good and the wind should be light but favorable for the run to Curacao. They waste no time in setting the sails. Gabby then slips into the cockpit to enjoy the late-night sail, while having a cup of hot chocolate with marshmallows on top, her favorite. The island looks like it is Christmas time, with the lights blinking in and around the town. As they move down the west side of the island, the bright lights give way to darkness. Lisa and Susan are up ahead about four-hundred yards. Gabby hears the radio come to life, and its Susan. "Gypsy Wind, come in." Gabby picks up the radio and replies, "Go ahead, this is Gypsy Wind." "Gabby," Susan says with excitement in her voice, check out the Witch's Hut! There's a light in the window!" Gabby takes the binoculars and starts scanning the shoreline, looking for the house. "Wow! Granddaddy, there's a light in the window of the Witch's Hut!"

Jack takes the binoculars and has a look for himself. "Well, what do you know?" Jack shakes his head and says, "Looks like the old witch is out tonight." "That is so strange," Gabby says. "When you told us the story the other day, you said that fisherman had reported seeing a light in the window when coming past the house at night on the way back in and that they offered a prayer." "That's what I told you and that is how the legend goes."

**THE WITCH'S HUT**

Gabby sits quietly thinking of the story, then says a simple prayer that the father found his baby girl ok. Jack keeps an eye on Lisa's stern light. They are moving along at about the same speed, but Jack is always aware that he might overtake her without noticing it.

All of a sudden Jack sees Lisa take a hard turn to port, for no apparent reason. He can hear what sounds like a yell and the crash of the boom slamming hard, echoing across the water. All of a sudden the danger is crystal clear. A sail boat has passed Lisa and is now bearing down on Gypsy Wind, dead ahead. The boat is without running lights and is on Gypsy Wind before they know it. Jack makes a hard turn to starboard, throwing Gabby on the deck of the cockpit, where she hits her head on the ship's wheel. The unknown sail boat passes within twenty-five feet of Gypsy Wind, and Jack can clearly see the three men on deck. After passing the boat, Jack looks for the name on the stern, but it looks to be covered up with duct tape or something. It appears the boat is running under full power with no sails.

After returning back to the previous course, Jack helps Gabby back onto the cockpit seat. Gabby is shaken but ok, after the ordeal. Jack calls Lisa. "Is everything ok up there?" Lisa replies, "I think so. He didn't hit us, but he came real close. Maybe I could have seen him if we had some sort of a moon tonight, but with their black hull and no sails or running lights, they were on me before I knew it. How about you?" "We're ok," Jack answered. "I had a little more time to react, thanks to you. Gabby did hit her head, but she's alright. Why in the world would anyone be running without lights?" "I don't know," Lisa replied, "unless they were up to no good. Were you able to get the name of the boat?" "No I'm afraid not," Jack said, "they had it covered up." "Well there you go," Lisa stated. "They were up to no good." Lisa and Jack resume their course and head for Curacao. Lisa's customers are busy changing their clothes after spilling hot coffee all over themselves as well as the galley. As for Susan, she was sitting next to the main mast, and she weathered the mishap ok. She is thinking to herself, "Could this be connected to the Witch's Hut, from going inside the house?"

The rest of the run was rather easy and they reach Curacao without further incident. They drop Lisa's customers off, then resume their trip to Puerto La Cruz.

Gabby can't get the Witch's Hut and the light in the window out of her mind. "What could it mean, and how could it happen? Could the story and curse be for real?"

Later in the night, back on Bonaire, a pickup truck pulls off the road and two figures jump out and start unloading packages wrapped in plastic. They store the parcels under the bushes which over hang the sand at the water's edge. The truck continues on down the road, leaving the two men with the cargo hiding in the underbrush.

A light blinks just off shore, from a dark shadow which resembles a boat of some kind. The three men onboard notice that lights are visible on shore now, indicating their pickup location. One of the men pulls a dinghy alongside the sailboat and jumps in, starting the outboard. A second man joins him and they head toward the lights that lead them to their landing spot. There is no moon and the coastline is completely dark, except for the lights glowing on the hill side. Pulling the dinghy up on the sand, one of the men hiding in the underbrush comes out to help steady the boat as two pirates climb out. "Have you got the stuff?" one man asks. "Yeah, we got it," answers another. "How about you?" "Yeah, the money's here." "Well let's see it!" "Not until I see the goods." Moog tears one end of the bundles open so the buyers can inspect the bills. Satisfied, the pirate reaches into the dinghy and hands over a briefcase with $100,000.00 dollars. The transaction is complete and the two buyers return to the boat with eight bundles, containing two million dollars of U.S. currency in counterfeit $100 dollar bills. The fake money will slowly reach the United States. Moog and Wonka cross the road and hide out while waiting for the truck to return and pick them up.

# Chapter 10

It is late afternoon, and Lisa and Jack have navigated their way to the entrance buoys outside of Puerto La Cruz. Lisa takes the lead. She has made many trips here in the past for fuel and supplies. They tie up at the fuel dock, where an officer stands dressed in black pants, white shirt, and a white hat. The officer goes over their paperwork and passports while making notes in his wire bound notebook. He walks up and down the dock, looking each boat over thoroughly. He collects the entrance fee and directs them to the fuel pumps.

The group plans to spend the night, and then head back to Bonaire the next day. Lisa fuels up first, then Jack follows. "Jack, take this fuel filter," Lisa offers. "That's Ok," Jack replies, "I have one of my own." "Good," Lisa says. "If you don't use filters you might find yourself with bad fuel." After fueling up, Jack and Lisa move their boats to two anchor buoys in the harbor.

"Hey," Jack suggests, "Let's head in for dinner and check this place out." "Sounds good to me," Lisa replies. "The last time I was here there was a little restaurant just to the left of the fuel pumps. I guess it's still there, its been about five months since I've been over."

Puerto La Cruz was founded by the Spaniards in 1600. The port has the look of early Spanish architecture, which is also reflected in some of the older buildings that line the main street.

 After locking everything down, the four head in for dinner. "This place looks a lot like the place we stayed at last year, off the coast of Georgia," Gabby says to Jack. "In what way?" he asks. "Remember how old all the buildings looked? And they were right on the street, just like these are." "Well," Jack replies, "My guess is they were built around the same time frame." As the four walk down the narrow street, an oxen cart makes its way toward them, down the center of the street. The sounds of hoofs and large wooden wagon wheels, grinding their way into the cobblestone and finely crushed gravel, echo up between the one and two story buildings that line each side of the street. The four move to one side to allow the cart to pass. An old man wearing sandals, tattered overalls with no shirt, and a straw hat stained with sweat walks behind and off to one side of the cart. He is carrying what looks to be a long bamboo stick, about five feet long.

He uses it to tap the hind quarters of the beast from time to time, motivating it to continue.  As the oxen passes Susan, it turns its head and snorts at her.  "Susan," Gabby laughs, "I think he likes you."  Susan laughs as well then says, "Great, that's just what I need.  A big cow chasing me down the middle of the street in a strange town.  Well it's not a big cow but I get the idea anyway."

Located down a side alleyway, with doors wide open and music drifting out, they four arrive at the little restaurant where Lisa had eaten on her last trip.  A quaint little restaurant, it is what might be called a hole in the wall.  With pink and gray exterior walls, and paint flaking off, the restaurant (or cantina as some might call it), is at the end of the ally.  The outer walls seem to be stucco.  The steps are wooden and match the two double doors, which are pulled wide open to let the evening breeze that is whipping down the alleyway into the building.  The owner walks over and welcomes them in Spanish as they reach the front door.

Gabby and Susan return his greeting before Jack and Lisa can reply. The owner leads them to a table. Jack and Lisa sit back and let the girls take control of the conversation. The grown ups know a little Spanish, but not to the extent that Gabby and Susan have mastered it.

Looking around the room while waiting for her meal, Gabby notices two locals sitting at the bar. The men have no shoes, and they are wearing long tan pants covered in what looks to be paint spatters. Both are sporting tattered t-shirts, with ball caps on their heads. The two men keep looking at the four cruisers. Gabby, being aware that they must be talking about them, thinks, "I guess they don't see that many tourists off the beaten path, and this place is definitely off the beaten path for sure." The smell coming out of the kitchen is of fresh bread, and all four comment to the owner how good the aroma smells. "Yes, would you like to buy some bread?" Jack looks at the girls who are nodding their heads in agreement. He turns to the owner and says, "Yes, that would be nice. How about you Lisa, do you want some bread?" "Boy, it sure does smell good. Why not?" Lisa answers. The owner bounds off to the kitchen with a smile on his face.

"That was one of the best meals I've had in a long time," Jack states. Susan laughs as she points out, "I'm glad I'm on Lisa's boat tonight." "Why is that," Gabby asks. "Did you see how many refried beans your grandfather ate?" "I may be sleeping on the deck tonight!" Gabby says, as Lisa laughs out loud. Jack responds, "Ok you three, how about cutting me a little slack?" "Granddaddy, we were just joking. But I think I'll sleep on deck anyway." Jack shakes his head.

The group thanks the owner for the wonderful meal, and for the bread, which he has wrapped in brown paper that looks a lot like butcher paper. Walking towards the door, Gabby turns and takes one last look at one of the men at the bar, who has been watching them throughout dinner. She finds he is watching them as they leave as well. Gabby makes eye contact with the man. His gaze goes right through her. She also notices the other man is missing. After emerging from the restaurant, she sees the missing man leaning against the building holding a rusted old bicycle. She feels uneasy but safe, knowing there are four in her group. They head back to the boats for a good night's sleep, and their departure the next day.

Later that night, Gabby, not being able to sleep, is lying awake in the vee-berth on Gypsy Wind. The winds are light and the night is quiet. She turns her head to the left to hear better. Something is outside and maybe on the deck. She has opened her forward hatch, hoping that a breeze might find its way into her cabin. She pulls herself to the top bunk and climbs out onto the bow without making a sound, but not before grabbing the flashlight which she always keeps next to her. There in the dinghy, which is tied to the toe rail, is someone she recognizes immediately, one of the men from the restaurant. He is trying to steal the dinghy! Gabby turns the flashlight on and yells at the same time, "Stop! Granddaddy he's stealing the dink!" Gabby yells at the top of her lungs, shattering the calm of the night. The man is sitting down at this point and has gotten the outboard motor running while Gabby is still holding the light on him. The thief puts the dink in gear and gives the motor full throttle. The bow of the dink points away from Gypsy Wind. Jack has awakened and is in the cockpit in time to witness the dink pulling away.

Gabby can't see the smile on Jack's face as the dink, running at full throttle, suddenly jerks to a stop, throwing the man from the boat and into the dark water.

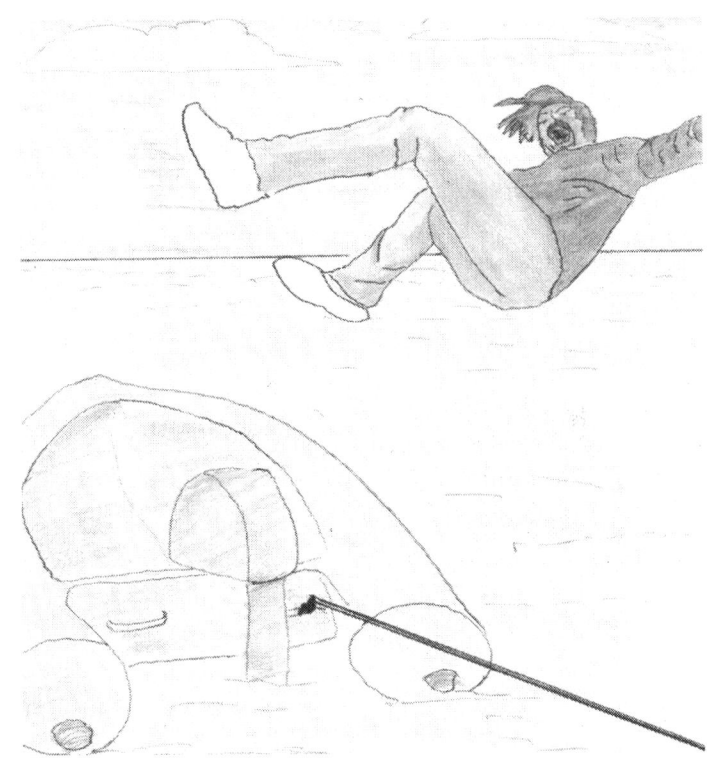

"Granddaddy, what happened?" Jack is laughing now, at the sight of the man flying headfirst over the bow of the dink, arms and legs going in every direction before splashing into the water. "Well sweathear,t I tied the dink off to the toe rail with a white rope that anyone could see. But I also ran a black cable from the transom of the dink to the stern cleat on Gypsy Wind, out of sight. He never saw it!" Jack is laughing as he watches the man still swimming for his life. The dink at full throttle ran about twenty-five yards before the slack ran out and the dink came to the end of the cable and a sudden stop. Gabby starts to laugh as well. "Granddaddy how did you know someone might try to steal the dink tonight?" "Well, today in the restaurant I noticed the two locals at the bar checking us out, so I thought I might build a little insurance into the locking of the dink tonight. It looks like it may have paid off." "Granddaddy, I saw the guys too," Gabby says. "That's good sweetheart. Always keep your wits about you when you're in unknown territory. Your mother used to travel a lot, and I would close each letter I wrote to her with the same phrase. "Sweetheart, be safe and keep your wits about you. Always know what's going on around you."

Jack pulls the dink back alongside Gypsy Wind and ties her off once again. He completes the night's sleep in the cockpit, just in case the thief should try again. Gabby returns to the vee-berth and finally drifts off to sleep. The next morning the radio comes to life and pulls Jack out of a deep sleep. "Gypsy Wind, come in." Lisa wants to know if Gabby had run Jack out of the boat and made him sleep in the cockpit last night. "Jack," Lisa says, "I knew those refried beans were a bad idea." Lisa and Susan are laughing while Jack shakes his head and replies, "I told you we might have visitors last night. You'd better check to make sure everything is still where you left it." Lisa stops laughing and quickly does inventory, finding everything in place.

The day is uneventful as they leave Puerto La Cruz, making their way back to Bonaire. Coming in from the north end of the island, once again they pass by the Witch's Hut. Gabby and Susan stop for a moment to look at the walls that remain, remembering the near disaster on the night of their departure, as well as the light glowing in the window of the hut, the same light which many other fisherman have told of seeing. They both think of the curse.

Could the old grandmother haunt the house still? Gabby and Susan can't wait to get back on the trail of the mystery.

## Chapter 11

Mrs. Cortes makes her way from the bedroom to the living room, talking to herself. "Now I know I have some photos somewhere, where did I put them?" She opens the closet door in the living room and finds a box on the top shelf. "Yes, this has got to be them," she says with a smile on her face. "Now, let's see what we have." Mrs. Cortes takes the box to the garden where she had entertained Gabby and Susan several days before. She has spent many afternoons sitting in the shade of the old tree, even as a child. It's nice to know some things never change, she thinks to herself. Sitting down and having her afternoon glass of juice, she opens the box which has a familiar smell of mildew about it. She slips her glasses on and pulls the first photo from the weathered green cardboard shoe box. After working her way through half of the photos, she says out loud, "I don't believe it." She has found a photo of Andrea and Carlos, but not one of the child. Reaching the bottom of the box, an image she has almost forgotten appears. It is a photo of her great-great-grandmother, surrounded by flowers on what seems to be her birthday, or maybe even the Festival of Dia Di. She looks at her watch and sees the time has slipped away while she was taking the long trip down memory lane. "I must get going. I need to run to the store for some things before dinner," Mrs. Cortes says out loud. She returns the box and the contents back to the shelf, except for the two photos that Gabby and Susan had requested.

Gabby and Susan make their way to the truck, leaving Jack with the chore of cleaning Gypsy Wind after the crossing. He offered to take care of the clean-up so that Gabby and Susan can go back to exploring the island. He didn't have to offer twice.

"I think we need to head over to Mrs. Cortes' house," Susan says. "I hope she was able to find some photos of the family," Gabby replies. "Me too," Susan agrees. The girls make their way to Rincon, and Mrs. Cortes' home. Arriving, they pull off the road just as they did before, across the street from her house. As they reach the front door, a man walks out from behind the fence which encloses the back yard and says in a gruff voice, "What do you want?" "Hello," Gabby is startled. "My name is Gabriella and this is Susan. We have stopped by to see Mrs. Cortes, would she be about?" "Why do you want to see her?" the man asks. Susan and Gabby look at each other with surprise. "Mrs. Cortes is helping us with some research we have been doing. Could I have your name please?" Gabby asks. "I'm Moog. I live here." "Nice to meet you," Gabby says, as a car pulls up to the back of the house. Moog sees his aunt, Mrs. Cortes, getting out of the car. He turns and walks around the corner of the house and out of sight without saying another word.

Mrs. Cortes comes in the back door and sets her groceries on the kitchen table, then proceeds through the house to the front door to greet the girls. "Hello, please come in. I was thinking of you two this morning. How have you been? How was your trip to Venezuela?" "Just fine thank you," Susan replies. "I saw you talking to my nephew, Moog," Mrs. Cortes says. "I hope he was nice to you." "Yes, very," Gabby says, as she glances over to Susan. "I found a photo of Andrea and Carlos, and I also found the only photo that I know of, of my great-great-grandmother Shania." Mrs. Cortes hands the photos to Gabby and she looks the photos over. The couple in the photo are standing together, with no expressions on their faces.

Gabby thinks, "Why didn't anyone smile back in those days?" She gets to the grandmother and sees the same expression, but notices that the women is dressed in what must be a beautiful dress.

Gabby thinks, "It's too bad the photo is in black and white. I'll bet that dress was so colorful."

While Gabby is looking at the photos, Susan notices Moog standing in the shadows in the other room eavesdropping on their conversation. "Tell me dear, what are you two wanting to know about the family and the little house? I can't remember what you said the last time you were here." "Well," Gabby answers, "we are doing research on the story behind the little house and what happened there for a paper we plan to do for school." Gabby is careful not to refer to the house as the Witch's Hut out of respect. "We want to know about the curse and the legend that surrounds the old house. We plan to go there today to take lots of photos of the home site, and the area around the house." "Well dear, I never go up there, and I suggest you stay away from it as well." Gabby smiles then says, "Everyone says the same thing, but we really don't believe in ghosts." Then she adds, "Would it be ok if we make copies of the photos?" "I don't see where that would hurt, but you must promise to bring them straight back to me," Mrs. Cortes says.

The girls thank her for her help and make their way out the front door. Crossing the street, they find Moog leaning up against their truck, right next to the driver's door. Moog looks at Gabby and says, "I suggest you two stay away from that old house, bad things happen to people that go around there." Moog stares at the girls. Gabby and Susan say nothing as they get in the truck, start the motor, and put it in gear. Moog moves off the truck as the wheels start to move. Gabby looks in the rearview mirror as they drive off. Moog is standing in the middle of the street, watching them drive away. His arms are crossed and there is a frown on his face.

"Gabby that was scary," Susan says. "You bet it was," Gabby agrees. "I would hate to run into him in some dark alley one night." "And where in the world did he get a name like Moog?" Susan wonders. They look at each other with expressions of relief as they go to make photocopies at a small office supply store (which doubles as an office machine repair business), just down the street from Mrs. Cortes' home.

Once the photos are returned to Mrs. Cortes, the girls are off to the Witch's Hut to make photos of their own.

Arriving at the Witch's Hut, Gabby parks the truck in the same spot Jack had chosen on the first day the girls had laid eyes on the house. They get out of the truck and head for the front door.

"Gabby," Susan says, "do you think it's smart to go back in after what happened before?" "Don't be silly," Gabby replies. "Almost being rammed by another boat and having the dink almost stolen had nothing to do with this old house." Susan persists, "Just the same, I don't feel good about this."

The girls enter the house for the second time in less than a week. Gabby walks into the front room and notices candle wax on the window sill. "Susan, come look at this," Gabby calls. "Candle wax on the window sill. What do you think about that? No self respecting ghost would leave candle wax behind." Susan reaches down and pulls some of the wax from the sill and smells it. "Smells strange," she says, as she flips the piece from the end of her finger. "Well, that explains the light we saw the other night as we passed the hut on the way to Venezuela." Gabby has a questioning look on her face. "Susan, someone is playing some sort of game, or trying to make people think the hut is haunted. Let's look around and see if we can find anything else." The girls walk out back and find a pathway which seems to lead into the bushes. Beyond the bushes is a steep cliff, eighty or so feet high. Susan kneels down and touches what looks to be fresh foot prints in the sand. "Gabby look at this! Footprints that lead into the heavy bushes. Nobody could walk through that stuff." After taking a few photos, the girls walk back to the truck, only to find all four tires flat. "Gabby, look, the tires!" Susan exclaims. "I knew we should have stayed out of that house. It's the curse!" Gabby shakes her head in disgust, then turns the radio on. "Gypsy Wind, come in." She repeats herself, "Gypsy Wind, come in." The radio comes to life with Jack's voice. "This is Gypsy Wind, go ahead." "Granddaddy, Susan and I need a little help if you don't mind, over." "What is it sweetheart?" Jack asks. "We have four flat tires on the truck." "How in the world did you manage to do that?" Jack asks. "It's an interesting story," Gabby replies. "I'll tell you all about it as soon as we get back." "You went inside the hut, didn't you?" Jack asks. "We'll talk about that later. Where are you?" Gabby keys the radio to reply. "We're at the Witch's Hut." Jack thinks for a moment. "I'll have to call the rental place and find out if they can run another truck out to you. For the time being, just sit tight. I'll call you back and let you know what's going on." "Ok Granddaddy, we're sitting tight. See you soon." The girls laugh as Gabby clips the radio onto her belt. They have no clue someone is watching and listening from the bushes, not twenty feet away.

An hour passes and the girls are getting bored, so they start to walk around. Gabby finds herself at the water's edge across the road from the Witch's Hut. As she scans the horizon, her eye finds its way to some underbrush. She sees something at the water's edge and she is compelled to bend down and pick it up. "A $100 dollar bill!

Susan, come look at what I just found!" Susan looks at the bill and says, "Cool, but look, some of the printing is missing. It looks like it washed off or something." They look at each other with a questioning gaze.

Safely back at the boat, Gabby and Susan can't wait to show Jack what they found. Motoring out to Gypsy Wind, Gabby sees Jack on the deck, hanging his solar shower from the main mast. Jack sees the girls and waves as they approach. "Hi girls, glad you made it back."   "Wait until you see what we found Granddaddy, you won't believe it."   Now standing in the cockpit, Gabby hands the $100 dollar bill over to Jack.  "What in the world have you two found?" Jack says as he inspects the half faded bill.  "Where did you say you found this?"  Susan answers, "On the sandy beach across the road from the Witch's Hut."  Jack settles down in the cockpit as he looks at the bill with a strange look on his face.  "Hold on one minute, I want to look at something."  Jack disappears down the main hatchway and soon returns with a $100 dollar bill.  He starts to compare his bill with the one the girls had found.  "Girls, do you know what you found?"  Jack looks at the two of them, and then answers the question before they have time to respond.  "It's a counterfeit $100 dollar bill.  It looks like half of the ink has washed off, but from what I can tell it's the best fake I've ever seen."  "Well, what should we do about it Granddaddy?"  Gabby asks.  Jack thinks for a minute, then picks up the radio and calls Lisa.  "Gypsy Wind to

Wanderlust, over." Jack calls once again before Lisa acknowledges. "Go ahead Gypsy Wind, this is Wanderlust, over." "Lisa, do you have a few minutes? I would like to show you something rather interesting, over." "Sure Jack. I was just getting ready to head in to shore, so I'll stop by on the way in." "Thanks Lisa. I'll see you in a few, over and out."

Lisa arrives and climbs onto the boat. "What's up, Jack?" Lisa asks. "Come sit down and have a cool glass of iced tea, and take a look at something the girls found." Lisa takes her seat as Susan hands her the glass of tea. "Thanks, Susan," Lisa says. Jack hands the bogus bill to Lisa. "Well Jack, you weren't kidding. Where did you girls find this?" Gabby recounts the events of the day at the Witch's Hut for Lisa. Jack asks, "What do you think we should do?" Lisa thinks, then says, "Jack about five months ago I met a guy from the F.B.I., he was down here on business. He never said what type of investigation he was conducting, but he stayed on the island for about a month. He and I got to be acquainted somewhat while he was here. He even made a run over to Venezuela for fuel with me. He wasn't a bad crew member either. I have his phone number in my address book. I think he was a little taken with me, and said if I was ever in Washington D. C. to look him up. His name is Special Agent Howard Dunlap." "Do you think I should say anything to the locals here about the bill?" Jack asks. "You know Jack, I think I would keep quiet about it and talk to Howard first. This is a small island, and if something like this gets out, no telling who'll find out about it." Jack smiles and says, "Thanks Lisa, that sounds like a good idea. Call me with his number and I'll contact him first thing in the morning. I'll let you know what he says."

# Chapter 12

Later in the evening a phone conversation continues. "Relax Moog, and tell me what's going on." Moog is excited. "I said I think they're on to us!" "Who?" the voice on the other end of the phone asks. "Those kids!" Moog shouts. "They have been snooping around the hut and they've been to my aunt's house three times now. They must know something!" "What kids are you talking about Moog?" the voice asked. "I don't know what their names are. I just know they were in a rental truck from Island Rentals, and they keep hanging around the hut and asking questions." "Ok," the voice replies, "I'll call Marge at the car rental and find out who they are. Then I want to see you tonight so we can get to the bottom of this. We don't need any problems now, we have the new plates set and will be ready to start printing." Moog shakes his head in agreement as he says, "See you tonight."

Later that night, Moog and Wonka meet at the back door to the customs office and knock. "Come in, and be quick about it," Officer Warzes says. "This had better be good. What is so important that it couldn't be handled on the phone, Wonka?" Wonka rubs his head before speaking. "Well, it's like this. Moog thinks we have a problem. There have been some girls asking a lot of questions, and they have been hanging around the hut. I checked with Island Rentals and found out they are two girls off a boat by the name of

Gypsy Wind, tied up in the harbor. Also their grandfather is on board, his name is Jack Elder."

Officer Warzes looks at Moog and Wonka and raises one eyebrow. "You two bone heads, this is what all the excitement is about? I've already met the girls, and they're just doing a paper on the hut for school." "Then maybe I shouldn't have cut their tires," Moog says. "You did what!" Officer Warzes shouts. "I was just trying to scare them off, like I've done to others before them." "Look," Officer Warzes says, "there is nothing to worry about. Just do your job, get the new bills started, and leave the girls alone." Moog stands up, but he makes no reference to the bill he saw the girls pick up, for fear of reprisals from the others. "Maybe it will come to nothing," he thinks to himself. "I never would have dropped the bill if they hadn't made me open the bag. How was I to know one fell out? It's not my fault," he thinks to himself.

The sun is slowly rising above the roof tops along

the shoreline as Jack sits in the cockpit, having his morning coffee. The fishermen are heading out for the day, which disturbs the tranquil anchorage as their wakes move past the boats and onto the shoreline. This is Jacks favorite time of morning, when he can be alone with his thoughts. He's thinking about calling Lisa's FBI friend. Jack knows something is going on regarding the fake $100 dollar bill, and he feels a sense of loyalty to his country to report it. He thinks to himself, "I'll make the call after my morning coffee. They should be up and about in Washington by then."

Jack dials the phone and waits for an answer. "Federal Bureau of Investigation, may I help you?" the voice on the other end of the phone asks. "Yes, my name is Jack Elder, and I need to talk to Special Agent Howard Dunlap. Is he available?" Jack feels the delay in the transmission, which is common in overseas calls when using the satellite phone. "As a matter of fact he just came in. I'll connect you, please hold on." Jack waits, then hears the phone ring. "Agent Dunlap, can I help you?" "Hello, my name is Jack Elder. I'm calling from the island of Bonaire. A friend of yours, Lisa Wilkerson gave me your number." "Of course, Lisa," Agent Dunlap says. "How is she doing?" "Very well, and she said to tell you hello," Jack replies. "She is a very interesting lady," Agent Dunlap says. Then, with the pleasantries out of the way, he continues. "Mr. Elder, what can I do for you this morning?" Jack explains, "My girls have found something on the island that I think might be of interest to you, and Lisa said I should talk it over with you before talking to the locals." "What might that be?" Agent Dunlap wants to know. Jack replies, "They found a counterfeit $100 dollar bill, which I think was printed on the island. Some of the ink was so fresh it had washed off at the water's edge, where the girls found it." Jack waits for a response, but the agent is silent for a long moment before speaking. "Mr. Elder, please do me a favor and do not contact the locals regarding the bill. We have an investigation on-going in that region. I can't tell you more than that now, but you may have stumbled onto the break we have been hoping for. I'll be heading to the island on the next available flight. Where can I find you?" Jack is surprised at the agent's reaction. "I'm anchored next to Lisa's boat. Do you remember where that is?" Agent Dunlap answers, "I sure do. Tell Lisa I'll give her a call as soon as I hit the island. And Mr. Elder, the fewer people that know I'm coming, the better it will be. Do you understand?" "Got it," Jack replies. The two men end their conversation and Jack settles back in the cockpit, wondering what he and the girls have gotten into.

Chapter

14

Special Agent Howard Dunlap steps off the plane and heads through customs. He had forgotten about the heat the little island could produce in the summer months, until he walked through the doorway of the jumbo jet. Emerging from the baggage claim area, he spots Lisa, who is there to pick him up. "Lisa, how good to see you again," Agent Dunlap is smiling. "I sure have missed you," He puts his arms out. Lisa wraps her arms around him while giving him a big hug, accompanied by a kiss. It is easy for observers to tell the two are more than just friends by the intensity of the hug and duration of the kiss. "Come on Howard," Lisa says, "throw your bags in the truck and let's go. You can stay with me on Wanderlust, if that's ok with you." "Lisa that sounds great," Howard replies. The fewer people that know I'm here the better. And it will give us some time together as well."

Lisa and Howard make their way to the waterfront. After parking the truck they head to Lisa's boat. As they dinghy out to Wanderlust, Howard asks, "Where does this Jack Elder anchor?" "There, right next to us," Lisa points at Gypsy Wind. "Well, that is convenient", he thinks to himself.

After settling in, Howard says, "Let's run over to Mr. Elder's boat. I would like to see the bill, and have a long talk with him." "I'll give him a call on the radio and see if he's aboard," Lisa says. "Wanderlust calling Gypsy Wind, come in, over." Lisa waits for a response.

F.B.I. AGENT
HOWARD DUNLAP

She repeats the call.. Jack picks up the radio and responds, "This is Gypsy Wind, go ahead, over." Lisa says, "Turn over to channel sixty-nine please, over." Jack obliges and turns the dial to the requested channel. "Hello Lisa, what's up?" Jack asks. "Jack, I have someone I would like for you to meet, do you mind if we come over?" Jack replies, "I don't mind at all, but who is it?" Lisa looks at Howard as he shakes his head from side to side, preferring she not say his name over the radio. "It's a surprise, Jack. We'll see you in a bit." Lisa flips the radio dial back over to sixteen out of habit.

Jack starts picking up some clutter in the main cabin, preparing for his guests. "Gabby, Susan, Lisa is coming over with a guest she wants us to meet. I think it might be the F.B.I. guy from Washington. Why don't you two straighten up the v-berth a little before they arrive?" The girls work quickly and soon the v-berth is as neat as a pin. Jack hears the distinctive sound of Lisa's outboard as it comes along the port side of Gypsy Wind. "Hi Lisa. Come aboard, and bring your friend," Jack hails. "Jack, I would like you to meet Howard Dunlap. Howard, this is Jack Elder, his granddaughter Gabby, and her friend Susan." "It is very nice to meet you all. I came as quickly as I could after talking with you, Mr. Elder." "Please, call me Jack." "Ok Jack," Howard agrees. "Could we go below and talk? I would like to see the bill you found." Jack replies, "The girls found the bill out by the Witch's Hut the other day, but yes, let's go below."

Jack returns from his cabin with the bill and hands it to Howard. Jack, Lisa, Gabby, and Susan wait for his response as he pulls another bill from his pocket for comparison. "It is a dead-on match." Howard is excited. He looks up and adds, "We have been seeing more and more of these bills showing up in the states over the past year, but until now we were not sure of the source. I was here some time back because we had a tip that they might be coming from Bonaire, but after about a month with no luck, Washington pulled me off the case." Howard continues, "If you don't mind, I would like to know everything about the day you girls found the bill. Lisa has already told me about the near collision." The girls recount their every step that day, leading up to finding the bill. Agent Dunlap is pleased with the new lead and invites the group to dinner later on that evening.

That night, Jack and the girls head for the dock to meet Lisa and Agent Dunlap for dinner. "Howard, this is very nice of you to invite all of us to dinner," Jack says. "My pleasure Jack," Howard replies, "do you have a favorite place you like to eat?" "Well," Jack thinks for a moment then replies, "not really. We seldom eat out. Maybe Lisa should choose." Lisa thinks for a moment then suggests, "I know a place where we can have a little privacy and talk. The food isn't bad either. Let's head over to the Lion's Den, I think steak is the special tonight." "That sounds great," Howard replies. The group drives over to the restaurant and finds a table overlooking the water, while a band plays island music on the dock below next to the bar. "This is really nice," Jack says. "You know, I once stayed next door to this place while on a dive trip."

Agent Dunlap changes the subject, wanting to get right to the business of knowing more about the night they saw the candle in the window of the Witch's Hut, and the day the girls' tires were flattened. "I'm sure the Witch's Hut is involved in some way, but why would there be candles in the window on some nights but not every night?" Howard takes a drink of water as though it will render the answer. Gabby speaks up. "You know, the locals think the Witch's Hut is haunted, and no one ever goes around there. We've had more than one person tell us we had better stay away from that place or bad things might happen." Susan cuts in, "I don't know about haunted houses and such, but as far as I know ghosts can't light candles. And Gabby and I saw some wax on the window sill of the hut. But ever since we went into that place we've had nothing but bad luck so maybe it is haunted. I don't know anymore." Lisa speaks up, "Howard, you know those mountains behind the hut are filled with caves." Howard shakes his head then replies, "Yes, and I think I might have to do a little exploring tomorrow to see what I can find. Lisa do you know where I can find a four-wheeler to rent?" Lisa answers, "There is a rental place just around the corner from the food store down town. I'll run you over there in the morning before the day heats up. It gets really hot up there in the afternoon."

Gabby and Susan do not see Customs Officer Warzes sitting in the booth next to theirs, and the group continues to talk freely. Officer Warzes recognizes Agent Dunlap from his last trip to the island, and she knows why he's here again. Concerned, she picks up parts of their conversation, then dials her cell phone to alert the others that trouble is once again on the island. "Agent Dunlap must be stopped", she thinks to herself. "But how?"

## Chapter 15

It is early morning and Lisa motors Howard in to shore, so that he can get to the four-wheeler rental center. He wants to get an early start due to the heat, and he knows the longer he's on the island the word will get out that he's here. He is afraid that things will change before he has a chance to discover what's going on.

"Yes, I'll need it for a half-day," Howard says as he stands at the rental counter. He fills out the proper paperwork and is given instructions on how to use the four-wheeler.

A local standing at the counter asks where he plans to ride. "I think I'll do some of the back trails up around Witch's Hut. I hear there are lots of trails up there with some very nice views." The local replies, "Yeah, lots of trails in that area. Would you like me to give you a lift? I just dropped my four-wheeler off for repairs and I'm headed back that way. I'll be more than happy to run you up there. You'll have to drive back though." "Man, that's great, thanks," Howard says.

Howard and the man load the four-wheeler onto the trailer and the truck slowly pulls out of the driveway. "I don't think I got your name," Howard says. "Sorry about that, just call me Moog." "Nice to meet you Moog," Howard says, "and thanks again for the ride." "No problem, man," Moog replies. They are nearing the Witch's Hut, and Moog keeps driving right past it. "Hey Moog," Howard says, "you missed the hut. Or do you know a better place to unload the four-wheeler?" "Yah man, I know a better place." Moog turns and smiles. Howard looks over and realizes that Moog is pointing a gun at him. "What is this all about, do you plan to rob me?" Howard asks. "Well Mr. F.B.I. man," Moog replies, "you and I are going to take a little ride. I don't want to kill you if I don't have to. If I were you, I would sit tight and behave." Howard realizes he's been compromised.

Moog enters the preserve on the north end of the island, and turns off the main road that runs through Washington-Slagbaai National Park. The road is bumpy and riddled with potholes. Howard thinks of making a move for the gun, but stops. "Maybe I'll play it cool and see what happens," he thinks.

He sees an old shack overlooking what seems to be a point, marking the end of the island. He knows they are in the middle of nowhere, with nobody else around. "Ok, out of the truck, "Moog demands. Howard opens his door, moving slowly. They walk to the front door of the shack, with Moog bringing up the rear. Once inside, Howard is told to sit down. Moog pulls three zip ties down off a shelf and ties Howard's hands behind his back, almost cutting the circulation off. Howard yells, "Hey, not so tight!" Moog says nothing as he ties Howard to the bunk beds that are in the room. "That should keep you!" Moog turns and points the gun at Howard and says, "Maybe I should kill you right now." Turning his head as if wondering what to do, he says, "No, not today." Moog smiles and heads back to the truck. Howard can hear the truck as it drives away, bouncing over the potholes, heading for the main road.

The afternoon is passing and Lisa waits for Howard to call. She was planning to pick him up in town at noon. Now, at 2:00 p.m., she is starting to get worried. She motors over to Gypsy Wind. "Jack, would you ride into town with me? I'm getting worried about Howard. He's not back yet." "Sure," Jack answers, "I'll be happy to. Where do you want to start?" "I think the rental center is a good place." Lisa and Jack pull up to the rental center and walk in. The man at the counter greets them and asks, "Can I help you?" Lisa speaks. "Yes, I'm looking for Howard Dunlap, he rented a four-wheeler this morning. Has he returned it yet?" The man looks in his books and replies, "No not yet. He should have been back at noon. You know I'll have to charge him for the whole day now." Lisa looks aggravated at his comment. "Let's go Jack. Something is wrong, I can feel it." Jack and Lisa head for the Witch's Hut in hopes that they will find Howard, but they have no luck finding him or the four-wheeler. It is almost dark when they return to the rental center to check one more time. The four-wheeler has not been returned. "Lisa, I'm not sure what to do. Howard is a professional in this sort of thing, and he may not want us to talk to the police yet." "Well, I can't just sit around and worry. I have to do something," Lisa says with a look of desperation on her face. "I'll tell you what," Jack says. "If Howard hasn't checked in by morning, we'll put in a call to

Washington and talk to his boss." "Ok Jack," Lisa agrees, "I'll wait until morning. God, I hope he's all right." Lisa settles back in the cockpit with a glass of wine, a worried look on her face. She knows there will be little sleep for her tonight.

As darkness descends on the little shack, Howard realizes he can't break the tie wraps which hold his hands. In total darkness he settles back, wondering what Lisa is thinking now that he has not returned. He's not worried for himself, he has faced danger before. His concern is for Lisa, should she get involved. "These people will stop at nothing," he thinks. "I don't want her to get hurt."

Morning comes with no word from Howard. Jack and Lisa decide to wait about contacting Washington. Instead, they go into town to file a missing person report with the police. The police station is quiet as they walk to the high counter where a uniformed police officer sits. "May I help you?" the officer asks. "Yes," Jack speaks first. "We would like to file a missing person report please." "Ok, I can help you with that. Please fill out this form with the name and description of the person in question." The officer pushes the paper across the table. After Jack and Lisa complete the form, the officer reads the description out loud. He turns and calls another officer over. "This is very interesting, a four-wheeler." the second officer says with a perplexed look on his face. He looks at Jack and Lisa and relays information. "Mr. Elder, a four-wheeler was found on the other side of the island. It was rented from the same place your Mr. Dunlap rented his." "Well that's something," Jack says. "Where was it found?" Jack waits for the answer. The officer looks at Jack and Lisa for a moment, then answers. "The four-wheeler was found at the base of a cliff overlooking the ocean. The distance to the water must be at least thirty meters." Lisa's face goes blank with the news. Jack pulls his composure together and asks, "Did you find a body?" "No." The officer breaks eye contact, and says, "The currents are very strong in that area." The officer assures Lisa and Jack that if anything is discovered, they will be informed at once. They walk from the police headquarters in a state of shock, not knowing what to do next.

Gabby and Susan wait impatiently on Gypsy Wind with the radio. If Agent Dunlap comes back, they are to contact Jack and Lisa with the news.

"Susan, do you remember the trail I found out in back of the Witch's Hut, that stopped at the bushes?" "I remember," Susan says. "But I'm not sure if I like where this is heading." "What do you mean, where it's heading?" Gabby asks. Susan explains, "After last summer in Webster Point, I'm surprised your grandfather allowed us to come back this year at all." "Don't worry Susan, we'll stay out of it this time. I've learned my lesson. But still, I'll bet that trail holds the clue to this mess."

## Chapter 16

"Moog, you idiot, no one told you to do that!" Moog sits quietly while Officer Warzes walks back and forth in her office. "What are we going to do now?" she asks, her face just inches from his. "We'll have every F.B.I. agent in the United States down here looking for this guy." "I had to do something. The guy was planning to run the trails up around the cave. He was sure to find it, it was just a matter of time." Warzes thinks out loud and says, "I just hope nothing comes of all of this. The police are buying the accident story. That's the only thing you did right, you moron. The currents are so strong in the area where the four-wheeler ran off the cliff, they will never look for a body there. It's just too dangerous."

Warzes continues. "I want the operation closed down after the next pickup. The tanker will be back on Friday, and after that we're down for a while. Things are going to get hot around here, and I'm not talking about the weather. It might be a good time to take a vacation off the island, if you know what I mean." Moog looks at Warzes, then at Wonka, and asks, "What about the F.B.I. guy?" Warzes answers, "Moog, he only saw your face, so let's keep it that way. Where do you have him?" Moog replies, "He's in the little cabin I built up on the preserve. No one ever goes up there."

Wonka speaks, "You know, there is an old abandoned tugboat up at the fuel facility. I think it might be a good idea to move him over there. Maybe

Captain Salvador can take him off our hands. You know, for a little swim about a hundred miles off shore." Warzes agrees, "Ok. Move him. But do it quickly."

After Moog leaves, Warzes turns to Wonka and says, "Wonka, make sure Moog keeps a good eye on that F.B.I. agent. The last thing we need is for him to get loose." She then repeats, "The agent has only seen Moog at this point, so let's keep it that way." Wonka suggests, "You know Moog could be in big trouble. He's an idiot. It might be a good idea for Moog to disappear, when the time is right, along with the F.B.I guy." "Wonka, don't do anything until you talk to me," Warzes instructs. "That's how we got into this mess in the first place. People trying to think, and they don't know how! Just get the shipment ready by Friday, and I'll run it to the tanker. In the meantime, I'll come up with something."

Back at Gypsy Wind, Lisa, Jack, Gabby, and Susan sit in the cockpit, wondering what to do next. "I'm not just going to sit here and do nothing," Lisa exclaims. "It looks like the police believe he ran off the cliff, and they're not even trying to find his body." She starts to cry. "Lisa," Jack says, "first of all, I don't think he ever ran off the cliff. He had no reason to be on that side of the island. He had planned to run the trails up around the Witch's hut. If we are going to find him, it will be somewhere around the hut. I'll bet on that." Gabby decides to break her silence. "Granddaddy, do you remember last summer, up in Webster Point Georgia?" "All too well sweetheart," Jack answers. Gabby continues, "As I recall, you told Susan and me that we should stay out of it and let the police handle it." Jack lowers his head and says, "You have a great memory. But this is a little different. You and Susan are going to stay out of it." Gabby laughs as she looks at Susan and says, "Right."

Agent Dunlap has been missing now for two days. Lisa and Jack have contacted his office in Washington

D.C. and were told nothing other than the Bureau would take care of it.

Jack and Lisa head to the police station one more time, to try to get the investigation started, but they have no luck. "This is going nowhere. Let's head up to the Witch's Hut," Jack suggests. The two get into Lisa's truck and drive to the hut. Arriving around 7:00 p.m., they park next to the house. Walking inside, Jack sees the candle wax in the window sill and points it out to Lisa. "Jack, come back here," Lisa calls. Lisa points to the trail that Gabby and Susan had told them about. "It does stop just inside the brush," Lisa says. Jack looks in and around the area, then pulls on a rope which is attached to a large section of underbrush. As he pulls, the underbrush starts to move away, revealing the rest of the trail. Jack looks at Lisa and raises his eyebrows. The two make their way up the trail and find two more brush piles blocking the way. Jack moves these out of the way in the same manner and they continue on.

Jack sees tire tracks in the sand as they make their way up the trail. He knows they are from a four-wheeler, but he doesn't know if they were made by Agent Dunlap. Once at the top the trail, they stop in front of what looks to be a cave, with a camouflage curtain over the entrance. Jack looks at Lisa and she nods her head. He pulls the curtain open. No one seems to be around, so the two walk inside.

Jack and Lisa scan the area slowly. The air has the smell and feel of dampness and mildew, but it also has a strong odor of ink and alcohol. Lisa walks over to a wooden table and picks up a hand full of $20 bills, holding them up for Jack to see. As Jack looks at the bills, he sees a look of terror come over her face. He soon realizes her fear as he feels the muzzle of a shotgun at the back of his head.

"Well, well, what do we have here?" Moog walks around from behind Jack, then motions for Lisa to come over. Moog asks, "What do you two think you're doing up here?" "Nothing, we are just sightseeing, that's all," Jack says. Moog looks at Lisa and says, "You two wouldn't be looking for a certain F.B.I. man would you?" Lisa can't contain herself and says, "Do you know where he is? Is he alright?" Jack rolls his eyes. Now Moog knows why they are here. "Come with me," Moog orders, "I'll take you to him." Moog takes Jack and Lisa down the hill to his truck, and forces Jack to drive to the main gates of the fuel facility and to the tugboat where Agent Dunlap is being held.

Moog called Wonka when the trio left the cave, telling him to meet the truck at the gate to the fuel facility. "Wonka, I have two more for the tugboat." "You have what?!" Wonka yells. "That's right, I have two more, so just shut-up and get over here, now." Wonka calls Warzes with the bad news. "Warzes, Moog has kidnapped two more people that were up around the cave." "Wonka, that's not funny," Warzes says with a worried voice, "You'd better be kidding me." "I'm afraid not," Wonka replies. "I'm on the way over now to unlock the gate and help put them away for safe keeping." Warzes can't help but say, "Wonka, you're right. We might have to send Moog on a little trip as well. He's the stupidest I've ever seen, and he's going to drag us down with him."

Once Jack and Lisa are on the tugboat, Lisa runs over to Howard and wraps her arms around him. "I thought you were dead!" "No I'm alright," Howard assures her. Jack now understands that their relationship is more than just a friendship. Moog pushes Jack in the back with the shotgun, telling them both to sit down. Moog and Wonka tie Jack and Lisa up with tie wraps. Wonka is wearing a ski mask. Moog asks, "Wonka, where in the world did you find a ski mask on Bonaire?" Wonka looks at Moog thinking, "You idiot, you just told them my name!"

As Moog starts to leave he looks back at the trio, wondering what he's going to do with them.

## Chapter 17

It is 10:00 p.m., and Gabby and Susan are sitting in the cockpit of Gypsy Wind, waiting for some word from Jack and Lisa. Gabby has called her grandfather a number of times on the radio, with no luck.

"Gabby what should we do?" Susan asks with a tremble in her voice. Gabby looks at her and says, "I'm not sure, but we have to do something, and quick. Let's get the truck and ride up to the Witch's Hut, and see if Lisa's truck is there." "Good idea," Susan agrees, adding, "We'll need a couple of flashlights."

The girls dinghy over to the dock. It is now 10:30 .p.m. The dock is bustling with people at the bar. Music drifts across the waterfront as if nothing is wrong. However, Gabby and Susan hear only the sound of their hearts beating as they start the truck and pull out onto the roadway, heading for an unknown danger.

Arriving at the Witch's Hut, they find no sign of Jack and Lisa. They have been missing now for three to four hours. "Where could they be?" Gabby asks. Susan shakes her head with a bewildered look on her face. The girls walk all around the area with their flashlights, but find nothing.

"Alright Susan, we need to head back into town, put our heads together and come up with a plan." Susan agrees as Gabby turns the truck around. Susan has seen this look on Gabby's face before, and she knows that things are about to get crazy. "Just like last summer in Webster Point," she thinks to herself.

Later, sitting at the bar having a coke, Gabby starts thinking out loud. "Ok, let's look at what we have. We know a counterfeiting ring is operating on the island. We know that Agent Dunlap is missing because of it, and he went missing up around the Witch's Hut. Now Granddaddy and Lisa have disappeared in the same area. We know someone has been putting a light in the window of the hut to scare people away, making it seem haunted." Gabby is on a roll and continues. "You know Susan, I'll bet that light had something to do with the boat that almost ran us down on the night we left for Venezuela. He was running without lights, like he wanted to be undetected." Susan speaks up, "You know, you're right Gabby. That's where we found the counterfeit money, too." Gabby states, "Everything points to the Witch's Hut. We've got to head back up there tonight and do a little sightseeing, if you know what I mean." "You're right, Gabby,"

Susan agrees then adds, "What about calling the police?" "Not a chance," Gabby says. "We don't know who we can trust."

## Chapter 18

"Wonka, I think it's time for that vacation I talked about," Warzes says into the phone. Wonka protests, "What about this mess Moog has got us into? You want me to take care of Moog and the F.B.I guy?" "No!" Warzes says firmly. "Not yet, do you understand?" "Ok," Wonka agrees, "but when?" Warzes continues. "Wonka, we are going to make so much money on this next shipment, we'll never have to work again. We'll split Moog's share and head for

Venezuela, and just leave him to deal with the F.B.I." "Sounds good to me," Wonka is smiling on the other end of the phone.

Meanwhile, out at sea, the Venezuelan Crescent lumbers through the water on its way from Venezuela to Bonaire, for its regularly scheduled delivery of supplies. Captain Salvador is looking forward to taking possession of a profitable package, to be delivered by Warzes. He is unaware of the events unfolding in Bonaire as he nears the island paradise.

Moog is hard at work in the cave, completing the printing of the last of the counterfeit money. Wonka walks in to check on Moog's packaging progress. "Moog, help me put the bundles on the four-wheeler," Wonka requests. Moog walks over to help gather the bundles and sees Wonka drop his cellphone. "Wonka you dropped your cellphone." "Thanks," Wonka replies, "I can't seem to keep the thing on my belt. The hook is broken." Wonka picks it up and sets it on the table, then continues loading the bundles of money onto the four-wheeler. "Moog, I'm going to take the money down to the van. You start disassembling this place. When I get back, I don't want anything left that might lead the authorities to us." "Got it," Moog says, "I'll take care of it." Moog turns and goes back to work. Wonka starts the four-wheeler and heads down the trail with over ten-million dollars in counterfeit money, money which will net he and Warzes a comfortable retirement while Moog takes the heat.

Moog is cleaning up when he sees Wonka's cellphone lying on the table. He starts to run outside, then realizes it's too late. "No matter," he thinks to himself," I'll give it to him later."

Twenty minutes later, a cellphone rings and Moog pulls his phone from his pocket to answer. It takes him a second to realize that the ringing is not coming from his phone, it is coming from Wonka's. He then reaches for Wonka's phone and answers the call. "Hola," he says. The voice on the other end is Warzes. She does not recognize Moog's voice, she thinks she's talking to Wonka. Moog says nothing as she continues to talk, taking command of the conversation. "Listen Wonka, you were right. Moog and the others must die. They know too much and Moog is an idiot, he would tell everything. We could never live in peace as long as Moog is around. I want you to take care of all of them, and put their bodies over the cliff at the same place where Moog ran the four-wheeler over. Do you understand?" Moog, trying to change the sound of his voice, says, "Si." Warzes continues. "I'll deliver the money to the tanker, then meet you tomorrow night down by the salt pier at 10:00 p.m. I have a sailboat picking us up, and we're off to a new life. Remember Wonka, over the cliff, not on the tanker as we talked about earlier." Warzes hangs up and so does Moog. Moog sits down to take in the conversation he has just had with Warzes. "What a fool I've been," he thinks to himself. "They are going to steal my share of the money and hang me out to dry. Well, we'll see about that!"

# Chapter 19

In the still of the night, a light breeze drifts across the road from the water's edge. The moon is almost non-existent, which brings heavy darkness to the secluded stretch of road. Gabby and Susan have parked their truck up the road and walked back down to the Witch's Hut, where they are kneeling beside one of the burned out walls. They are hoping something might happen to shed some light on this mystery and lead them to her Jack and Lisa.

"Susan, listen, do you hear that?" Gabby whispers. "Yes," Susan answers in a low voice, "it sounds like a four-wheeler or a motorcycle." The girls can hear it, but they see no head light. "Look!" Gabby points at the underbrush behind the Witch's Hut as it starts to move, revealing a four-wheeler being ridden by a man dressed in black. The four-wheeler is loaded down with something. The man drives past the brush pile. Then he gets off the four-wheeler and replaces the underbrush back into its original position.

Gabby and Susan slip into the shadows inside the walls, making sure they can't be seen. The man pulls the bike out onto the road, then turns on his headlight and slowly moves toward town. Gabby says, "Let's follow him." The girls jump up and run back to the truck. Gabby finds running without headlights can be rather tricky as she maneuvers her way through the curves. Just when she thinks she's lost the four-wheeler, she spots movement off the road at one of the dive site parking areas. Pulling over, she and Susan get out of the truck and make their way to the dirt entrance, hiding behind the underbrush. The man is loading something into a white van. Gabby is trying to make out the name on the side of the van, but it's just too dark. "Susan, can you make out the name on the side of the van?" "No, I can't make it out." Gabby looks over the bushes and see the man starting the van and beginning to roll toward the entrance. The girls slip deeper into the brush as the van pulls past them onto the road, once again heading towards town. Gabby and Susan are stunned as they read the name on the side of the van door: "Bonaire, N.A. Customs Authority." "Let's get back to the truck," Gabby says. "I want to see what's up the hill behind the Witch's Hut." Susan nods her head in agreement as they emerge from the bushes. "Gabby, I cut myself all up in those bushes, they had thorns all over them." "Deal with it Susan, things could get worse later." Gabby turns and smiles, giving Susan that same devious look.

Heading back north, they park in the same place as before and walk back down the road to the Witch's Hut. Moving carefully up the hill while removing the underbrush obstacles in their path, they soon find themselves in front of what looks to be a cave. "Susan look, there's a light on inside," Gabby whispers excitedly. Susan points and whispers, "Someone is moving around inside." "Yeah I see them!" Gabby answers. "Now what?" Susan asks.

Moments later, the lights go out and Moog pulls the curtain aside. He stops and looks around as if he knows something or someone is there. After hesitating for a few seconds, he walks behind some bushes. Gabby and Susan hear another four-wheeler start up. Moog pulls onto the trail and makes his way down toward the Witch's Hut. The girls are lying on the ground behind a tree, and Moog is unaware of their presence.

"Let's go in and see what's in there," Gabby says. Susan protests. "Gabby, I don't think that's a good idea." "Quit whining," Gabby states, "and let's go." Gabby takes the lead and pulls the curtain aside. With her flashlight, she finds the overhead light and turns it on. She is amazed to see printing equipment. After uncovering the plot by his partners to kill him and take his share of the money, Moog had not completed his work. He had other things to do before the night was through.

Gabby and Susan start looking around for anything that might give them a clue as to the whereabouts of her Jack and Lisa. She spots a shotgun on one of the tables, and she picks it up. She had been bird hunting a few years ago with her paternal grandfather, on his farm in Chile, and she knows how to handle a gun safely. She breaks the gun down to see if it is loaded. It is, and she thinks to herself, "This could be useful later." She snaps the barrel back in place, locked and loaded.

Back at the customs office, Wonka pulls up to the back door. Warzes meets him as he is walking in and asks, "Have you taken care of them?" Wonka looks at her with a puzzled look on his face. "What are you talking about?" Warzes repeats, "Did you take care of Moog and the F.B.I. guy?" "No, you told me not to do anything until I heard from you." Warzes replies angrily, "We talked an hour or so ago you idiot, don't you remember?"

Wonka has no idea what Warzes is talking about. "I went off and left my phone at the cave. I didn't miss it until I was half way to town." "Well," Warzes wants to know, "who did I talk to?" Warzes looks at Wonka as she realizes what she's done.

Wonka asks, "What did you want with me?" Warzes regains her composure then says, "I want you to take care of Moog and the F.B.I. agent, as well as the others, but not on the tanker. Take them to the place Moog put the four-wheeler over the cliff. Then meet me tomorrow night at the salt pier. I have a sailboat picking us up at 10:00 p.m." Warzes now has no intention of hanging around till tomorrow night. She realizes she has inadvertently tipped off Moog to their plan, and he will more than likely be waiting for Wonka to make his move. If things work out, they will take care of each other and she'll be home free. Wonka pulls his knife. Holding it up as though he's looking forward to killing Moog and the others, he says, "I'll take care of it, right now!"

Gabby and Susan are still at the cave, looking around for more clues. Gabby finds Wonka's cellphone on the ground where Moog had thrown it. She picks it up and looks in the directory. Playing around with the phone, she is able to find only three numbers saved, two of which belong to Warzes and Moog. "Susan, remember the scary guy we met at Mrs. Cortes' house in Rincon? The guy named Moog?" "Yes, I remember him," Susan answered. "Who wouldn't?" Gabby continues, "I think his number is in the speed dial. Look, it says Moog. How many guys on the island could have a name like Moog?" Gabby calls the number and Moog, miles away in town, answers the call. He knows by the display that it is Wonka, his double-crossing partner, who must now be back at the cave. Moog answers, pretending everything is ok. "Hola." Gabby, not knowing what will happen next, decides to take a chance and speaks. "Moog, is that you?" Moog is perplexed to hear a woman's voice when he is expecting Wonka instead. He hesitates to answer, then says, "Who is this?" Gabby plays a hunch and says, "I'm the one who knows who you are and I will be coming for you soon if I don't find the three people that are missing. I also know about the customs office as well. I know everything about the counterfeit money, and if I don't get what I want, you and the others are going to pay dearly." Moog is dumfounded and does not know what to say. "Moog I'm waiting!" Gabby raises her voice. She is not sure if the ploy will work, but at this point they are out of options. She also knows the longer they wait, the less chance they have of finding her grandfather and Lisa alive, not to mention Agent Dunlap.

Moog is worried and his voice betrays him when he says, "Is this the F.B.I.?" Gabby thinks for a moment then replies. "Yes. I'm here with five other agents. We've discovered the cave and we will be picking up the others within the hour." Moog opens up and says, "I'm just the little guy, Warzes is the brain. All I was hired to do was cut and pack the money!"

Gabby can't believe what she is hearing. She says with a firm voice, "Where are Agent Dunlap and the two other people?" Moog answers quickly, "They're ok. Wonka had me take them to the fuel facility. They're being held in an old tugboat on the far end of the dock, but they're ok. I'll take you there, just understand I had nothing to do with all this, I was just the hired help. Wonka and Warzes were the ones." Moog is taking this opportunity to put as much blame on the other two as possible. He thinks, "I'll hang them out to dry, those two-timing backstabbers." He mistakenly thinks he is talking with the F.B.I. Little does he know he is speaking with Jack's sixteen-year-old granddaughter. "Ok Moog, I believe you. Where can we meet?" There is no answer from the other end. Gabby repeats the question, but still there is no answer. Unknown to Gabby and Susan, Wonka has arrived and has a knife to the Moog's throat. Wonka says, "Old friend, I think we need to take a ride. But first we need to stop and pick up some company for you. We wouldn't want you to be all alone, now would we?"

Gabby and Susan now know where Jack and the others are being held. "Susan, let's go back to the boat and get the scuba gear. I think we're going to need it."

After collecting the scuba gear and driving up to the fuel facility, Gabby parks the truck out of sight, near the unattended rowboats they had found a few days earlier.

The main gates to the fuel facility are locked. The girls can see a tanker at the dock, with workers on deck busily unloading cargo. The tug, where Jack and Lisa are being held, is barely visible beyond the stern of the tanker.

The girls assemble and don their scuba gear, and slip into the water at a dive site called the Windjammer, the site of a sunken ship. The old mast is still visible in the shallows, but the actual wreck lies far below the surface, beyond recreational diving limits.

The girls work their way carefully along the shallows, and come to a drop off. They know the deep water means the dock is nearby. In the early morning light, Gabby can make out the gigantic hull of the tanker looming in the distance. She can hear noise coming from the tanker, along with slight vibrations in the water surrounding the hull. Gabby thinks it is more than likely pumps making the noise. Little does she know that Captain Salvadore has given the order to prepare for departure, and the noise she hears is the hum of the power plant that moves the gigantic tanker. Making their way around such a large ship is a little unnerving, especially when they reach the large propellers. Should the propellers start to turn, the girls could be sucked into the blades and cut up, much like a kitchen blender might make short work of a piece of fruit. To the girls' horror, they now realize the hum they hear is the sound of engines deep within the tanker's hull. The propellers start to turn slowly in reverse. Gabby and Susan swim for their lives as they feel the pull of the current made by the cavitation of the huge props. Gabby notices a braided rope hanging off the bow of a tugboat up ahead. She makes a last ditch attempt and grabs the line, then quickly turns and puts her hand out for Susan, but Susan is nowhere to be found.

Gabby thinks in horror, "She's gone!" Knowing there is nothing she can do, she decides to pull herself along the side of the boat to the stern, and farther away from the pull of the props on the tanker.

As Gabby makes her way out of the current, all she can think about is Susan. She is surprised and relieved to see Susan making her way around the other side of the boat. The girls' eyes meet and each can see the look of relief in the other's eyes. Susan luckily found a cable running under the dock on the other side of the tugboat, and started working her way around that side. By the time Gabby made it to the rope and looked back, Susan Gabby is sure they are at the right boat. She can tell the old tug is in bad repair. was out of sight.

The hull is made of wood, and some of the caulking is starting to come out from in between the planks. "It's a wonder this thing is still afloat," Gabby thinks to herself.

The girls find tires hanging off the rails, all along the tugboat. The boat was used for pushing ships, and the tires were used to protect both hulls at the same time. Gabby takes her slate and writes Susan a note. "Let's stay close to the hull, take the scuba gear off, and hook it to something. We should be able to climb up by using the tires." Susan nods her head indicating that she understands the plan.

The Venezuelan Crescent sits at the dock, with the last of the cargo offloaded. Captain Salvador eagerly awaits Customs Officer Warzes and her very valuable package.

He wants to get underway as soon as she arrives. Warzes arrives at the dock with the counterfeit money packed in five bags the size of large ice coolers. She boards the tanker and makes her way up to the bridge, where the captain awaits her arrival. "Officer Warzes, it's good to see you again." Warzes answers, "Captain, there have been some last minute changes." "And what would those changes be?" the Captain inquired.

Warzes replies, "I need passage to Venezuela, to accompany the shipment." The captain states, "This is rather unusual." Warzes counters his comment with the statement, "It's unavoidable." She makes up a story to cover the reason for leaving the island. "Our buyer wants the local contact to accompany the shipment." Captain Salvador thinks for a moment then says, "Not a problem we have an extra stateroom available, which you may use for the crossing." Then the captain barks, "Crewman, come here. Follow the Officer to the dock and unload the packages. Put them in my cabin, and then show the Officer to the empty stateroom on deck three. We should be getting underway within the hour." He then looks at Warzes and says, "Perhaps you can join me for dinner." Warzes thanks the captain, then disappears down the ladder, making her way to the dock to retrieve the packages.

A little later, the Venezuelan Crescent slowly pulls away from the dock, making its way back to Venezuela. Warzes readies herself for dinner and a relaxing night, having made her getaway with the money and leaving Moog and Wonka to fight it. After dinner she sits on deck enjoying the night breeze, thinking about what she plans to do with her new-found wealth.

## Chapter 20

Jack, Lisa, and Howard sit in the cabin of the tugboat, thinking of what they might do. All three have duct tape across their mouths and cannot communicate with each other. Jack hears someone on the deck. The early morning light is making its way through the half-broken and dirty porthole. He can see the cabin door slowly opening. The three are not sure what to expect next, and none of them can believe their eyes when the door is fully open.

Gabby and Susan stand in the cabin doorway wearing black wetsuits and smiles. Jack makes a sound from under the duct tape as Gabby starts removing his gag and the tie wraps that are cutting into his wrists. Susan and Gabby get everyone untied, and Jack asks the obvious question. "How did you know where we were, and how did you get here?" But there is no time for answers. The five are about to head out onto the deck of the when they hear a voice and footsteps on the deck. "Gabby, Susan, everyone, get forward," Howard demands. Howard positions himself next to the cabin door, out of sight. The first person through the door is Moog, followed by Wonka, who is holding a knife against Moog's back. Howard has the knife from Wonka before he knows what is happening. The two men fall to the floor. Moog steps back, startled at what has just happened. Jack reaches down and grabs the knife Howard knocked from Wonka's hands, and once again Moog can feel the point in his back. Howard has Wonka down and he yells for Lisa to hand him the rope that is hanging from the ceiling of the room. Moog can't stop talking. "I was here to let you go, I really was. I talked with the other F.B.I. agents and told them I would bring you three safely back. I'm working for you now. Warzes and Wonka made me do all the other stuff." Howard pushes Moog and Wonka through the cabin door and down to the dock where the pickup truck is parked. Then he ties their feet together. The tanker has been gone for some time now, and no one is around. The crews designated to work the ships leave shortly after unloading the cargo. A skeleton crew stays on to watch after the facility.

There is hardly enough room in the pickup for the group, even though it's a full-sized truck. Making their way back to the police station, Moog can't stop talking to Howard, who is in the bed of the pickup with him and Wonka. "I'm telling you, I had nothing to do with all this. Wonka was going to kill me too!"

It is daylight, and the girls have not slept in what seems like days. All of them have arrived at police headquarters. The police take Moog and Wonka into custody, as Moog continues to protest. Moog is yelling even louder, "I'm supposed to be let go! I talked to the F.B.I agents! You have it all wrong, I was the one helping the F.B.I."

Gabby and Susan start laughing as Moog is dragged away to the back room that holds the cells. Jack asks, "What was that all about?" "Well Granddaddy, you just met the dumbest crook alive. Susan and I talked to him on the phone and told him we were F.B.I. agents." Howard looks puzzled and asks Gabby, "Where are the rest of the agents?" Gabby smiles and says, "Mr. Dunlap, there never were any other agents. Susan and I made that up to trick him into cooperating. That's how we knew how to find you all. We even told him we would let him go if he helped." Gabby and Susan giggle. "Wow, do you two need a job?" Howard asks in jest. "This guy sure filled my ears up with what has been going on. It looks like the customs agent got away a little while ago, with a lot of counterfeit money, on that tanker headed for Venezuela." "How do you know she was on the tanker, Howard?" Jack asks. "Well, this Moog character said something about a sailboat, but I noticed the customs van left unattended on the dock at the fuel facility. That makes me think she's on the tanker. I'll get in touch with Washington and have her picked up when they dock, along with the captain. I'm sure he's involved in this mess as well. The Venezuelan authorities will be more than happy to help. The United States is doing a lot of trading with Venezuela right now, which makes them more helpful in situations like this.

    The police take statements from everyone and then allow them to leave, hopefully to enjoy a shower and a good long sleep. Jack looks at the girls and gives them a big hug. "You know, I must be the luckiest man in the world to have two of the greatest kids in the world. I think you two could do anything once you set your mind to it." Gabby smiles and says,

"Granddaddy, you always said if you believe you can do it, you're right, and if you believe you can't, you're right. You taught us to believe in ourselves, and the rest will fall into place." "Well sweetheart, you may have saved all our lives by using your wits and quick thinking. I do love you dearly, and that means both of you. Now let's head to the boat, I'm tired."

Everyone sleeps late the next morning. While Jack is having his morning coffee in the cockpit of Gypsy Wind, he notices movement on Wanderlust. It's Howard, who raises his hand and waves. Shortly afterward, Lisa appears and sits down with Howard. All seems well again, as Jack sits watching the little waterfront stores slowly come alive. He can't get the girls off his mind.

Later that day, they all return to the bar on the dock, for dinner and the free sunset over Klein Bonaire. They are all recounting the events of the last few days, when two gentlemen approach their table. Howard looks up and asks, "Can I help you gentlemen?"

"Would you be Special Agent Howard Dunlap?" the first man asks. "Yes, I am Agent Dunlap," Howard replies. The man pulls out his identification, indicating that he, too, is an F.B.I. agent. "Agent Dunlap, we were told you were missing and we were dispatched down here to locate you, as well as to find out what was going on." Gabby and Susan look at Jack, Lisa, and Howard, and start laughing while the two agents look confused. Howard says, "Gentlemen, we're sorry for laughing. Please pull up a chair and have a seat. We have a very interesting story to tell you. Would you care for some dinner?"

Meanwhile, Wonka sits in jail thinking, "There is a sailboat waiting for me at the salt pier. Warzes is waiting for me, wondering where I am. Is she aboard the sailboat?" Little does he know she's on the tanker headed for Venezuela, and never intended to meet him. There never was a sailboat.

# Chapter 21

Jack is planning to run the girls over to Aruba for a few weeks, for a little sailing and some shopping. Gabby and Susan have been shopping for supplies all day, while Jack tops off the water supplies with the onboard water maker he installed before leaving the states. He checks the fuel supply and finds plenty for the crossing, thanks to their earlier run over to Venezuela some weeks before.

The Festival of Dia Di in Rincon is coming up the next day, and everything will be closed. Jack plans to depart on the day of the festival. Lisa told him the island would look deserted due to everyone being in Rincon. Gabby and Susan return with the supplies and start loading them into predetermined locations, which will make finding the items much easier later on.

It is the day of Dia Di, as well as Gypsy Wind's day of departure. Gabby asks Jack, "Granddaddy, would you mind if Susan and I run up to the Witch's Hut one more time before we return the rental truck?" "Go ahead," Jack replies, "but please don't go in the hut. You know it is bad luck." "Granddaddy," Gabby laughs, "you don't believe all that stuff, do you?" "Well sweetheart," Jack replies, "I guess I'm guilty as charged." Gabby rolls her eyes as she looks over at Susan, then says, "You know, the candle in the window and the whole story was made up to scare people away from the hut because of the counterfeiting ring." "Maybe so," Jack agrees, "but just the same, stay out of the hut. Please."

The girls make their way up the narrow road to the Witch's Hut and park next to the little cottage. They walk over to the front door, but they do not enter. "Gabby," Susan says, "you know the candle was only there to scare people away. But Andrea did die in the house, and her child was taken from her. We also know the great-grandmother did live in Rincon." "I know," Gabby acknowledges, then adds, "Susan, do you know what today is?" "Yes," Susan answers, "it is the Festival of Dia Di, over in Rincon." Gabby looks at Susan, then says, "Not only is today the day of the festival, but it also the anniversary of the day that Andrea, was killed. Remember, Carlos was gone to town to sell their handmade goods when the men came ashore from *The Black Veil*."

"Gabby, I remember, but you don't really believe the story of the curse on the pirates and the house do you?" "I don't guess we'll ever know if the curse was real or not," Gabby agrees, "but the story will make a great paper for sure." The girls walk across the road and down to the water's edge where they had found the counterfeit $100 bill in the bushes. Susan and Gabby both look along the water's edge as if looking for another bill, but instead they see a wooden plank, like a piece of wreckage, floating in the water. Gabby reaches down and drags it onto the sand. "Susan, look at this!" Gabby has turned the plank over. The words "*Black Veil*' are carved into the wood.

Gabby looks at Susan and says with a smile, "The wreckage. Remember the great-grandmother's curse on the pirates and their ship? The name of the ship was *The Black Veil.*" At the exact moment she mentions the schooners name, a cold breeze sweeps across the sand from the direction of the Witch's Hut. The wind makes a sound that, for a second, resembles laughter, sending a chill over the girls' bodies, as if something or someone was there.

**THE BLACK VEIL WRECKAGE**

The girls look at each other, not knowing what to say.